Shadow

Aris Austin

Shadow

Copyright © Aris Austin 2016

This is a work of fiction. Names, characters, businesses, places, events and incidents are either the products of the author's imagination or used in a fictitious manner. Any resemblance to actual persons, living or dead, or actual events is purely coincidental.

Published by Austin Joseph

Denver, CO

ISBN 978-1540774941

Chapter 1

"Come on Shadow! Over here!"

Shadow shook the snowflakes from his coppery coat and turned to follow the sound of the man's voice. The man, a tall, pale human named Brian, led Shadow down the snow-covered driveway and toward the family car. Shadow wasn't exactly sure where they were going yet, but he had learned to trust Brian over the eleven years they'd been together.

Wherever they were headed, it was apparent that the new puppy hadn't been invited. He and the rest of the family were still inside, sound asleep. Whatever adventure awaited Shadow would be like the old days, after Brian had saved him from the dog shelter all those years ago. Before the marriage, before the children, before the puppy. Shadow loved the family, of course, but he *was* looking forward to having Brian's undivided attention again. Just the two of them. The thought was enough to make his tail wag.

Shadow paused at the curb, sniffing at the family's old Christmas tree. The tree had been in the house only a few days earlier, surrounded by presents, but had gone outside shortly after Christmas. Christmas trees did that every year.

Many Christmas trees ago, Shadow had delighted in eating prickly needles off of the lower branches, but now he was content to simply take in the smell. It reminded him of the endless forests he and Brian used to explore together.

"Shadow, come *on*!"

Shadow took one last sniff before hobbling over to the car, where Brian waited impatiently. Long ago, he would have run to the car with huge, bounding strides, but age had taken its toll on his bones and running just wasn't worth the joint pain. Fortunately, with age came patience. Shadow didn't rush, climbing into the car just one paw at a time before gently lowering himself into a seat.

Most days, Brian's wife Amy got to sit in the passenger seat, meaning Shadow had to share the back with Bri and Bel. Amy and the children were all asleep though, and the passenger seat was Shadow's for the taking. He panted excitedly as Brian ducked into the driver's seat, and nearly hyperventilated when the engine sputtered to life. A dog could see the whole world from the front seat of a car. That's what made it so special.

Brian swung the car out into the road, tires crunching over frozen patches of snow. Shadow stared through the window, watching the snow disappear beneath the car faster and faster, until the road was only a blur of white patches on black asphalt. Houses came into focus through the windshield, then shot by as quickly as they had appeared. Shadow whipped his head back and forth from windshield to window, drinking in the details of each speeding house.

When he grew bored with the houses, Shadow's attention turned back to Brian. Just the sight of the man brought on all the comfort and safety a dog could ever want. His pale face, covered in the scratchy stubble that tickled Shadow's tongue when he gave Brian kisses. The hard, gray eyes fixed firmly on the road. His fingers, all covered in hair— or, about as covered in hair as a human could get—that knew just the right way to scratch Shadow's favorite spots. Every bit of this man was familiar. Shadow had adored Brian's briny scent and low, quiet voice for nearly his entire life.

It was Brian who had rescued him from the shelter all those years ago. Brian who had taken him on long hikes or winter jogs; who had tossed scraps under the table for him; who always scratched the perfect spot while Shadow napped. They had been together long before the rest of the family came along, and as long as Shadow was in Brian's presence, he was a happy dog.

Although their love was the same, each of them had changed since their first days together. Shadow's knees had started to ache on cold mornings. Barely noticeable flecks of gray now dotted Brian's stubble, and prominent splashes of silver gathered at the end of Shadow's muzzle. Brian's nose had been straight when Shadow first met him, but in the intervening years, an accident had caused it to turn slightly to the left.

The day of the accident had been an icy day many years earlier, back when Shadow could still accompany Brian on his morning runs. Heavy snows the previous week had led to the removal of broken trees, revealing an overgrown trail off to the side of their normal running route. Exploring was the natural choice. Shadow raced ahead, off-leash as usual, nimbly leaping over thick roots and patches of ice. Brian had done his best to follow, but the poor human only had two legs instead of four. When a toe caught on a twisted root, Brian went flying forward, smashing face-first into the ice.

Shadow went back to his human's side immediately, howling for help until the man finally woke up. The pool of steaming blood beneath Brian's face was so large that for a few agonizing moments, Shadow had worried his human wouldn't wake up at all. Even though it was only a memory, Shadow couldn't help but whimper out loud. The idea of losing Brian was unbearable.

Brian took his eyes off the road for only a moment, staring at Shadow with concern. "What's wrong, buddy?"

He reached out to scratch Shadow's head, with a touch that had an instantly calming effect. *It's okay,* Shadow thought. *Brian's okay now. It was only a memory, and Brian is never ever going anywhere.*

Once they reached their destination—a small, poorly plowed parking lot—Shadow waited patiently for Brian to come around the car and open the door. Once the door finally did open, Brian knelt in front of it and scratched the back of Shadow's head. "Be good, alright?"

Condensation curled up from Brian's mouth, carrying the minty scent of gum with it. Shadow's only response was to give Brian's face a couple of licks, which tickled his tongue. Brian's stubble always tickled, but Shadow didn't mind it much. There was never a bad time for face-licking.

"Thank you," said Brian. He clipped a leash to Shadow's collar, which was confusing to say the least. *He hadn't worn a leash in years. Why did he have to wear one now?* Shadow trusted Brian though, and followed without hesitation when the man stood up. He padded through the parking lot at Brian's side, panting at the shiny new watch on his human's wrist. The watch was only a few days old, and had been a Christmas present, like the new puppy. Brian loved getting new toys, even when the old ones still worked. His old watch was probably sitting in some dark drawer, already forgotten. No doubt it would remain there for years, faithfully ticking away until its batteries finally ran out.

Good thing dogs were different from watches. Shadow lapped at a stray snowflake that landed on his nose, quickly forgetting all about the watch. The air tasted frozen today, almost as frozen as the snowflake. Brian looked uncomfortable in his thin jacket, but Shadow didn't mind the temperature. For some reason, the cold never fazed him. Maybe all of those long winter jogs with Brian had made him immune to the frozen air.

Shadow turned his attention back to the parking lot, trying to figure out why everything seemed so familiar. A nearby building with cracking paint looked so familiar he could almost smell it, but he still couldn't quite place it. It wasn't the vet. Shadow would have recognized the vet immediately. It could have been some new trail Brian wanted to try, since there *was* a trail snaking along behind the building. Brian wouldn't leash him for a run though, and he wasn't dressed for the cold. Shadow decided not to give it too much thought. Brian seemed to have a plan. Brian *always* had a plan.

Their destination turned out to be the familiar building with cracking paint. Brian held the door open, and the smell of the place hit Shadow the moment he stepped inside. He knew it from his earliest days, somewhere deep down in his memory. His nose wasn't quite what it used to be, but it worked well enough to pick apart most of the individual scents. There was the scent of cleaner on the floors, so strong it made Shadow wrinkle up his nose. The air carried hints of dog food too, but not the kind from home. Soap, concrete, dust burning in the filter of a poorly maintained space heater…each smell did little to mask the dominant scent in the air. *Dogs.*

The realization of where they were only confused Shadow more. He stared up at Brian, nervously swishing his tail from side to side. A woman seated behind a nearby desk started to speak, but Shadow interrupted her with an anxious whine. *Why were they back here? There was no reason to be back here.*

Shadow couldn't understand it. Dogs who had families weren't supposed to be there. It didn't matter that there were worse places for dogs to be. This was not a happy place. And when Brian had adopted him eleven years ago, Shadow never thought he'd see the shelter again.

Chapter 2

"How can I help you?" the woman behind the desk asked again. One of her hands rested on the keyboard of a computer, the other on a desk phone. She peered at Brian and Shadow through a thick set of glasses, almost suspiciously.

"Um, I have an adoption return," said Brian.

The woman snapped a form into a clipboard and stood up from her desk. "When was the animal adopted out?"

"Eleven years ago, in December," said Brian.

She hesitated, glancing at Shadow. "What's the reason for the return?"

Brian shrugged. "He's just getting too old and slow for my family and me. We're active, and we need an active dog who likes to run fast and play. I just think he'd be better off with someone who has a quieter lifestyle."

The woman stared at Brian for a moment, her mouth slightly open. She let out an exasperated sigh much too quiet for human ears, but more than loud enough for Shadow to notice. He wasn't certain he liked this woman. Her voice was too abrasive. Too cold and unfriendly.

"Okay well, we'll need to fill out this form," said the woman. "I'll take him into the next room for an intake assessment. What's his name?"

"Shadow," said Brian.

The woman nodded curtly and took Shadow's leash. "Wait out here."

She led Shadow through a door and into a room full of gleaming examination tables. A tall, thin man waited inside, dressed in a set of scrubs that weren't quite long enough for him. His hair, wiry and short, was a steely gray color that stood out in contrast with the deep brown of his skin. He glanced up as Shadow and the woman entered, revealing a dark, watery set of eyes.

"Hi Anthony. Intake," said the woman. "Some jerk out there decided to return a dog because he got too *old*. I've seen people like him before. Dump the dog when he's not 'fun enough' anymore. I almost let him have it right out there."

The man called Anthony removed a pair of reading glasses from his face and sighed. "You know you can't yell at people for bringing dogs here, Deb. But I know. Some people just don't seem to understand that dogs aren't toys."

Anthony spoke in a smooth, even tone that suggested he'd spent as much time conversing with frightened animals as with people. He shook his head slowly, then turned his gaze to Shadow. "Well, I supposed we can't do much about it right now. What's this guy's name?"

"This is Shadow," said Deb.

"Well, let's take a look at Shadow then."

He led Shadow to a scale and had him sit. When the scale chirped, Anthony turned to Deb and said, "58 pounds."

After Shadow stepped off the scale, the two humans lifted him onto an exam table. Shadow waited patiently while Anthony looked him over, deciding he liked the man. His voice had a calming effect. Every time he spoke, Shadow couldn't help but smile the classic dog smile: slightly open mouth, bright eyes, and tongue hanging out on the left side.

Anthony gave Shadow a quick pat on the back, and then spoke quickly while he conducted the intake exam. Deb gave Anthony no verbal indication that she heard, only nodding from time to time while she took notes about what he said.

"Brown eyes. Brown fur. Black nose and ears, gray around the muzzle. And his back paws are white."

He pulled Shadow's lips up and poked around. Shadow had to resist the urge to pull away. "Healthy teeth and gums," said Anthony.

Shadow ignored most of the assessment, blocking out the doctor's poking and prodding. Instead, he fixed his gaze on the door separating him from Brian. He knew Brian would be waiting on the other side of the door, just like any trip to the normal vet. Still, Shadow wanted to be by his human's side again. Even with Brian waiting just a few feet away, the shelter made him inexplicably nervous.

"His knees are a little stiff. He's an older dog, so might be he's developing a little arthritis. We'll watch his hips too."

Before he even finished speaking, Anthony wrapped his arms around Shadow's chest in an inescapable grip. He let go before very long though, and then stepped back to wave a hand in front of Shadow's face. Shadow tried his best to watch the hand, but the faster it went, the dizzier he got. He was almost ready to fall off of the table by the time Anthony finally stopped. "Good boy. No signs of fear or aggression, and no biting yet. Alright Shadow, time for a quick blood test."

As a puppy, Shadow had been terrified of needles. He'd been to the vet plenty of times over the years though, and stared ahead with stoic indifference while Anthony drew a vial of blood.

Anthony crossed to the other side of the room. Shadow expected Deb to follow, but she stayed put, still busy scratching out mysterious human letters onto her form. Eventually, she finished and set the form aside to give Shadow a few quick scratches.

His tail wagged with excitement. *He'd never met this woman before, but somehow she knew he liked to be scratched! Maybe she wasn't so bad after all!* Shadow leaned forward to lick Deb's face, but she ducked out of the way just before his tongue made contact with her glasses. Unfazed by the rejection, he flopped onto his side so Deb could rub his belly.

Anthony called over his shoulder from across the room, interrupting the belly rub. "Rapid heartworm test is negative. Go ahead and take him in. Oh, and put the guy leaving him here on the Do Not Adopt list."

Deb nodded and wrapped her arms under Shadow, lowering him back to the floor with a grunt.

"You're heavier than you look," she said. Then she straightened, adjusted her hair, and took hold of the leash. "Come on, Shadow."

Shadow followed Deb back to the lobby, pleased with how brave he'd been at the vet. Brian was always proud when he was brave, and a proud Brian made him happier than almost anything else. He waited as patiently as possible for the leash to be passed from Deb's hands back to Brian's, but that moment never came. Instead, only words passed between the humans, and then Brian knelt down to pat Shadow on the head.

"Bye, buddy."

Shadow wagged his tail nervously, unsure of what Brian meant. *He understood goodbye, but where could Brian possibly be going without him?*

Brian stood and thanked Deb. Then he turned and walked out the door without even a glance behind him.

Shadow decided he would be good. He decided that he wouldn't bark, or even whine. He simply stood rigid by the glass doors, watching Brian's distant figure climb into the car. And watching the car pull out of the parking space. And watching it creep toward the edge of the parking lot.

Shadow swallowed the whine rising in his throat. *Brian would come back for him.* He just had to be patient.

There was a tug on the leash as Deb tried to pull him away from the doors, but he refused to budge. Outside, Brian's car turned onto the road and gained speed.

Shadow felt vaguely aware of more pulling on his leash, but didn't give it much thought. He kept his gaze fixed on the corner where the car had disappeared, waiting for the return of his human. His Brian. His best friend.

Deb grabbed Shadow's collar while some unseen human pulled on the leash, forcing him to look away. They had to drag him for the first few steps, but after that he gave in and followed Deb through a new door. The new door led to a second door, which led to a long hallway lined with rows of kennels on either side. The kennels seemed large enough for comfort, but there wasn't exactly any room to explore. Most of them were occupied by dogs, some of whom barked at Shadow. Barking just for the sake of noise had always annoyed Shadow, but he tried not to let it get to him. Brian would be back soon anyway. He *had* to be back soon.

Deb opened the gate on an empty kennel and ushered Shadow inside. The kennel was arranged in a simple manner: food and water on the floor by the gate. A plastic bed in a back corner, along with a few blankets to offer some protection from the concrete floor's chill. The gate's chain links stretched from ceiling to floor, eliminating any chance of escape. The gate seemed almost ominous, but Shadow tried not to let it bother him. Brian knew how to open gates.

Deb knelt down and unhooked the leash from Shadow's collar. "I'm sorry that guy left you here," she said. "You don't deserve that. Don't worry though, we'll find you a new home in no time."

She folded the leash into her hand and gave Shadow a halfhearted smirk. "At least he forgot his leash, right? There's a little payback for him."

Deb stood and stepped out of the kennel, closing the gate behind her. As she disappeared through the door at the end of the hall, Shadow made sure to memorize the squealing of the door's hinges. He had no doubt that the squealing was important to remember. *That was the door Brian would come through, whenever he came back.*

****

One hour blended into the next, and by nightfall Shadow's bones ached from standing for so long. He'd started shifting his weight from paw to paw around late afternoon, which helped, if only temporarily. Later, when volunteers had come around to fill food bowls, he had tried to distract himself by eating. The food was all wrong though, and only made him homesick. While his normal food had a satisfying crunch, the shelter's food crumbled at the slightest touch. *Miserable.*

Why hadn't Brian come back yet? It made no sense. Someone *had* to come for him. Brian, or Amy, or maybe Bel, if the school bus ever stopped by the shelter. No one ever left him alone for this long, especially not in some strange place. Even when the family took vacations, Shadow went along.

The night dragged by slowly. Shadow waited, listening to the sounds made by strange dogs in neighboring kennels. He couldn't see any of them, except for the dog in the kennel across from his. She was asleep, just like she had been when he first arrived. She was much smaller than he was, and smelled younger too, although it was hard to tell with so many dogs around. Wiry brown fur stuck out from under the blankets at all angles, but Shadow could never fully tell what the sleeping dog looked like. She stirred once or twice during the night, but never left the blankets, and never noticed Shadow's presence.

Watching the other dog sleep all night made staying awake very difficult, and by the time the sun came up, Shadow could barely keep his eyes open. He finally decided to lie down, just to give his paws a rest, but not on the bed at the back of the kennel. Brian wouldn't be able to see him back there. Instead, Shadow settled down on the concrete floor and rested his head on his paws, nose inches from the gate. His eyelids grew heavier by the moment, and eventually fatigue won out over willpower.

It was a fitful sleep. Shadow woke up every time he heard a door open, hoping that Brian had returned. Every person who came through the door was a shelter worker though, or a volunteer, or the occasional family looking to adopt a dog. To make matters worse, some of the dogs in other kennels seemed determined to bark at everyone who came down the hall. Shadow tried his best to ignore them, but the only time the barking *really* went away was when he dreamed.

Brian wound his arm back and then whipped the ball forward, launching it halfway across the park. Shadow took off like a rocket, flying over the grassy terrain with ease. There was no need to watch the ball's path through the air; Shadow knew exactly where it was going to land, and looking up would only slow him down. He *never* slowed down when there was a ball on the loose, not even once it had landed. And he wasn't about to start. His jaws snapped together in perfect time with his feet, capturing the ball before it could bounce away. It never had a chance.

Shadow slowed to a stop and marched back to Brian, proudly padding through the soft grass. He let Brian's praises fall on him with an almost pompous air, and then dropped the ball on request. Within seconds, Brian had already thrown the ball again, and Shadow was racing after it.

On another triumphant march back to Brian, something caught Shadow's eye. A small patch of dandelions had taken root in the park, which was nothing special by itself. However, two of them looked different. Instead of bright and solid, they looked old. *And soft. Softer than socks, even.*

The ball rolled out of Shadow's mouth, forgotten. He leaned in to sniff the flowers, suspiciously stepped back, and then leaned in again. Brian called out, saying to leave it, and an older Shadow certainly would have trusted his human's judgement. The Shadow from the dream was much younger though, and curiosity won out over obedience. He snapped the heads up from both of the strange flowers in a single bite, crushing them between his jaws. Instantly, the dandelions crumbled in his mouth. They coated everything, finding their way to the space between his cheeks and gums, the bottom of his tongue, and the back of his throat. Shadow backpedaled, panicking. He shook his head violently from side to side, but the wet seeds refused to release their grip. *Why hadn't he listened to Brian?*

The gate to Shadow's kennel opened, and he was on his feet faster than an old dog ought to move. Instead of Brian's stubbly face though, Shadow met the gaze of a startled volunteer. She hastily dumped a scoop of food into his bowl and left, shutting the gate behind her as quickly as possible.

Was that the morning feeding, or the afternoon feeding? Disappointed, Shadow settled back down to the floor and tried to recapture the dream. He hadn't run that fast in years, and the dandelions seemed more amusing than panic-inducing now. Dreams allowed Shadow to revisit his younger body from time to time, and he missed the days where he wasn't limited by his arthritis. And he could visit Brian in dreams too, while he waited for the man's return.

It wasn't long before Shadow found his way into a dream again, but not of a day in the park with Brian. The new dream went further back, to a time Shadow didn't even know he remembered. He was only a puppy, and the entire world seemed full of wonder. Bigger. Newer. Shadow followed a long-forgotten woman through the shelter's parking lot, tripping over a set of paws much too large for his tiny body. The woman ushered him into the shelter's lobby, where he promptly flopped down to the linoleum and splayed his limbs out in every possible direction. Snippets of a hushed conversation between the woman and a staff member floated around above his head, but most of the words were lost to memory, made hazy by the years.

"…I still don't know how it happened, but she got pregnant… this little guy was the only one I couldn't find a home for."

"…we can take him, but I need to ask you to have your dog spayed so you don't get another litter of unwanted puppies… don't know how many dogs end up here because of that…there's a discount clinic on…"

"...No, we don't consider ourselves a no-kill shelter... very high placement rate though... puppy so he'll be just fine."

Shadow was taken into the same examination room and given the same physical exam, although the room looked much newer and Anthony was considerably younger. When he went back out to the lobby, the woman gave him a few treats.

"Bye puppy!" she said. Then she walked through the glass doors, just like Brian had.

And she never came back for Shadow.

Shadow woke with a start and struggled to his feet, blinking in the rays of winter sun streaming through the kennel's high window. The long-forgotten memory left an anxious feeling in his chest, an itch buried so deep inside that he'd never be able to scratch it. Shadow tried to hang onto hope, but it slipped from his grasp with startling speed. Realization could be cruel sometimes, and no amount of patience could prevent the pieces from falling into place. Brian wasn't coming back for him. Neither was anyone else. They left him behind, just like that woman had left him behind as a puppy.

The realization hurt. Shadow had barely known the woman from the dream, but Brian had been his best friend his entire life. And now Brian wasn't coming back. He'd been abandoned. *Betrayed.*

That was the moment when Shadow's heart broke.

Chapter 3

Age had weighed on Shadow's bones for a long time, but it was nothing in comparison to the crushing realization that Brian was never coming back. The unscratchable itch of anxiety in his chest suddenly vanished, replaced by a gaping hole. Shadow slumped down to the floor, certain his ribs would all cave in if he remained standing.

Cold had never bothered Shadow before in his life, but the concrete suddenly seemed to leech every bit of warmth from his body. He tried to whimper; tried to use his voice to find Brian and *make* him remember, make him once again love the dog he'd left behind. The sound caught in Shadow's throat though, choking him.

What had he done wrong? What made his family abandon him? None of it made any sense.

Facing reality was too overwhelming, so Shadow closed his eyes and waited for sleep. Sleep was the only way to escape the sense of panic that threatened to crush him at any moment. As soon as unconsciousness reached out for him, Shadow fell into its embrace for as long as he possibly could.

By the time he woke up, the hole in his heart had been replaced by a cool, dull ache. The sun had gone down, and all of the shelter workers had gone home. That was fine with Shadow. He didn't want any company.

The dog in the kennel across the hall was finally awake, and she greeted Shadow with a playful stretch. Even stretched out, she looked small—only half of Shadow's size, with pointed ears and fur that refused to arrange itself in any sort of organized manner.

On another day, Shadow might have returned the dog's greeting. If they had been at the park, they might have circled one another, sniffed back and forth, and gone off to play together. They were locked behind gates though. The people who took Shadow to the park were gone forever, and he didn't feel like making friends.

Shadow scooped a few bites of the crumbly food into his mouth, hoping it would make him feel better. In the past, he'd seen humans refuse food when they smelled of stress or worry, which had never made much sense to him. Being upset only made him hungrier. This time though, food did nothing to fill the pit in his stomach. It crumbled in his mouth like a dandelion, dry and tasteless.

Shadow tried one last bite, paused, and spat it out. Suddenly, food didn't seem all that interesting. He turned, walked the few short steps to the back of his kennel, and collapsed onto the bed. He didn't bother facing the hallway. *If no one was going to come for him anyway, what was the point?* Instead, he stuck his nose into the corner and put his back to the world. The whimper he had been trying to let out finally escaped his lips, but it wasn't anywhere near loud enough to bring Brian back. The sound came out weak and broken, which suited Shadow just fine. A broken voice for a broken dog.

Sleep didn't come to Shadow, despite the fact that he had absolutely no desire to be awake. *What point could there possibly be in staying awake?* The family he'd loved for so long had left him to die.

Shadow inched his body forward, pushing his face deeper into the corner. Perhaps dying in the kennel was exactly what he would do. He wanted nothing more than to lie on the bed, drifting in and out of consciousness until sleep finally won for good.

Lying there in the dark with his nose pressed against the wall, Shadow vowed two things. The first thing was not to move from the bed until the world finally slipped away.

The second was to never love a human again.

Chapter 4

"We don't know what to do with him. He won't leave that corner. I don't think he's eating or drinking. I don't think he's even pooping."

"You're sure he's not drinking?"

"His water has been full the whole time he's been here. I think evaporation can account for the little bit that's missing."

"Well… he was just fine when I checked him a few days ago. Might be he's just upset about being left here. Give him until this afternoon to see if he gets hungry or thirsty enough to get up. If not, I'll look him over and start an IV for the dehydration."

The owners of the voices stood just outside the door to Shadow's kennel, but he pretended not to notice them. He recognized one of the voices as Anthony, the vet from the day Brian left. The other voice had coaxed him to eat several times over the last few days, but he had simply ignored the human. He'd been making good on his promise to never leave the corner. He hadn't gotten up even once, at least not by his own free will. Someone had finally carried him to a common room the day before, in a desperate attempt to *make* him move. There were other dogs in the common room, and Shadow supposed they were meant to socialize, but he didn't care. As soon as he was let back down to the floor, he took exactly four steps to the corner of the common room and planted himself there. He kept his back to the other dogs until someone finally carried him back to the kennel.

Shadow knew they would probably try to move him again today. They could carry him to different rooms, but they couldn't make him eat or drink, and they couldn't make him play. Without food or water, his strength was already fading. That was alright with him. It wasn't that he necessarily wanted to die—he had seen death before, and it always confused and frightened him—but leaving the bed required an energy Shadow just didn't have.

As it turned out, no one carried him to the common room that day. Instead, someone entered his kennel around mid-afternoon and clipped a leash onto his collar.

"Come on, baby," said a woman. "It's beautiful out today. The snow finally stopped. Let's get you out for a walk and see if the sun helps you feel any better."

Normally, the word "walk" would have had Shadow on his feet in seconds. With Brian gone though, he ignored it as easily as he ignored the dust motes lazily drifting overhead. He also ignored the woman's tugs on the leash, which became more and more aggressive the longer he resisted. For a moment, Shadow wondered if the woman would drag him outside. That might be amusing.

Instead, he found himself lifted into the air by the same strong arms that had carried him to the common room. He hung limp from the human's arms in protest, but that didn't seem to make a difference. The floor floated by below, spinning on occasion as the human turned to maneuver Shadow through one doorway or another. The last doorway led outside, where Shadow was gently deposited on the ground.

"Maybe just being outside again will make him want a walk," said some unseen human.

Shadow still didn't want to walk, but being outside was certainly better than the kennel. The sun felt so good that he even decided not to get up and find a corner to face, so he simply stayed where he was. He barely even noticed the woman's series of attempts to get him up. Sadness had a special way of making the rest of the world seem far off, and the farther Shadow sank, the easier it got to ignore everything else.

The visit outside was short-lived. Once it was determined that Shadow had no intention of taking a walk, that strong set of arms lifted him into the air again. Instead of being returned to his kennel though, Shadow found himself deposited on Anthony's exam table. He did his best to ignore Anthony too, staring blankly ahead while the vet poked and prodded him. A vet tech Shadow hadn't met before tried to cheer him up, stroking his side and whispering things like, "you have *such* a soft coat" and "don't worry, we're going to make *sure* you feel better soon."

Blood was drawn, but Shadow didn't even feel the needles. Every inch of his mouth was checked, but even that didn't bother him. Anthony eventually declared that Shadow was in good health, and aside from severe dehydration, there was no medical explanation for his behavior. The vet's face came into view as he knelt down by the table, eyes full of concern. "What's wrong, big guy?"

Shadow turned away. Anthony used the same brand of shaving cream Brian did, and the traces of scent leftover from the morning made Shadow feel sick. He had eaten an entire tube of Brian's shaving cream as a puppy, and then vomited most of that same tube into Brian's open sock drawer. Even after all of that though, Brian had forgiven him. He'd certainly scolded Shadow, but there was never any talk of going back to the shelter. Shadow couldn't make sense of it. *What could he possibly have done this time? What made Brian mad enough to leave him behind?*

Anthony turned to someone out of Shadow's line of sight—probably whoever had carried him there. "My only guess is that he's devastated about being left here. Some dogs who get returned after only a few days take it pretty hard, and it sounds like he was with the guy that left him for most of his life. I haven't ever seen a dog react quite this badly before, though."

The vet shaved Shadow's forelimb and fitted him with an IV, carefully securing the catheter with tape. Shadow would have told Anthony that the tape wasn't necessary, that pulling it out would be too much effort, but humans were difficult to communicate with. There was no way he had the energy to get a point like that across. Instead, he watched the floor float by while Anthony carried him back to the kennel. Another human followed with a drip bag for the IV, which Anthony promised would help Shadow feel better. They left him on the bed with soft words and warm wishes, but Shadow immediately turned and deposited his face back in the corner.

A steady stream of people came by throughout the rest of the day. Everyone wanted to offer their love to the "poor, sad dog", scratching his favorite spots and speaking in those high-pitched voices usually reserved for puppies.

"It's gonna be okay, baby. We'll find you a new home."

"Look! I have some food in my hand! It's right by your nose. Do you want some food?"

"Hey buddy, if you roll over, I'll give you some tummy rubs. Would you like that?"

Shadow barely noticed the distant voices, and didn't bother to acknowledge them. He didn't want to love any more humans, and the depth of Brian's betrayal actually made that task quite easy. The IV slowly dripped away Shadow's dehydration, but it did nothing for the sadness. He fell apart a little more every time someone scratched his ears or patted his back, because the gestures only reminded him of the family he had lost. He was alone, floating in his own private ocean of despair. And all he wanted was to sink beneath the waves.

After the last reassuring voice went home for the night and there were no more humans around to hear, Shadow allowed himself a single, quiet sob.

Chapter 5

"Hey Anthony?" said a voice just outside of Shadow's kennel.

He recognized the voice. It belonged to someone from the parade of people who had been visiting him. There had been visitors more often than not since Anthony fitted him with the IV two days earlier, all of them petting him softly or pushing food in front of his face. Not that it really mattered. None of them could replace his family.

"Is it alright if I take one of the spare keys home tonight?" asked the voice. "I want to come back after I feed my dogs and get some dinner. I'm going to try and give this guy a little extra love after we close tonight, when it isn't so crowded. Maybe he'll eat a little something."

Anthony responded, but Shadow didn't listen to any of the specific words being said. Ignoring people had become almost automatic. A curtain of grief distorted their words, and only brief fragments of the outside world broke into Shadow's consciousness. He'd been vaguely aware of the sun coming up in the morning, and hazy memories of being carried to the common room occasionally floated through his mind. The dog from across the hall had tried to play with him, but eventually gave up. Shadow spent most of the day in the corner of his kennel, ignoring the barking of other dogs and the soothing voices of human visitors.

Sometime just after dark, the telltale click of the front door's deadbolt echoed through the shelter, signaling the staff's departure for the night. Shadow sighed in relief. He felt guilty for ignoring all the humans who tried to comfort him, but he couldn't help it. *Didn't they understand that Brian was gone? How could they tell him everything was going to be alright?*

As a puppy, Shadow had worried himself sick every time Brian left for work. He'd whine at the door for hours, staring and pawing until it swung open and his human finally returned. He eventually learned to trust that Brian would always return, but that trust had been misplaced. Only strangers came through the shelter's doors, and the only thing worth staring at was the back wall of the kennel. Shadow stared at the wall in the darkness the same way he did in the daylight; too tired to stay awake, but too upset to fall asleep.

Long after the other dogs had all gone to sleep, a woman opened the gate to Shadow's kennel and slipped inside. He hadn't heard her unlock the shelter's front door, which was odd because humans were normally so loud and clumsy. She took a seat on the floor next to Shadow's bed, filling the kennel with her scent. Every human had their own unique scent. Brian's had been something like sweat and sea salt. This woman smelled of unwashed hair, with a hint of dryer lint.

She sat in the dark for a long time, not saying anything. She didn't even try to convince Shadow to eat, which was a pleasant surprise. People dropping handfuls of food in front of his face had grown tiresome.

"Hey buddy," she finally said.

Shadow winced. "Buddy" was Brian's nickname for him, and he wasn't exactly ready to hear it again. He considered ignoring the woman, but her voice had a slightly melodic quality to it, each note gently floating into his ears. It was soothing, and quite different from the pitying voices of other visitors. Shadow decided to listen, at least a little bit.

The woman was silent for a moment. Then she continued carefully, as if speaking to a frightened puppy. "I hear your name's Shadow. I think that's a great name.

"You don't look much like a shadow though. Your fur isn't dark enough. Do you like to follow people around? Is that why you're named Shadow? I guess some people name dogs Shadow just 'cause they can, huh?"

She paused as if she expected a response. Then she said, "My name's Annie. Well actually, it's Anise, like the seed. I like Annie better though, so that's what I go by. Do you like aniseed? Maybe you've never had it. Wanna know a secret about it?"

She lowered her voice to a whisper, so only Shadow could hear. "I actually hate the way it tastes."

Annie laughed, a sound that made Shadow's ears prick up involuntarily. Her laugh was very different from Brian's laugh, or anyone else in Shadow's old family. It reminded him of the first birds that chirp after a rainstorm; hesitant at first, and then excited and shrill.

"Isn't that awful?" she asked. "I hate the plant I'm named after. To be honest, I kinda hate that it's my name. I mean, I guess it's a pretty name in theory, but the kids on the playground used to call me Anus instead of Anise, and I guess I never really got over that. I always laughed it off, but here I am fifteen years later, still hating my real name. That's okay, I guess. At least I like being called Annie."

She reached out a hand to pet Shadow's back. "You know, when I was a little girl, I had a dog who looked just like you. Her name was Penny, like the coin."

Annie laughed again, and Shadow couldn't help but feel a little warmth. "We had three cats and she was the only dog, so poor Penny lived her entire life thinking she was a cat. She'd always try to sleep on the back of the sofa, and she always looked so confused when she fell off!

"She'd try to follow the cats into cardboard boxes too, but she never seemed to notice that she didn't quite fit. I think the cats got a little irritated from time to time, because she kept flattening their boxes.

"Do you like cats, Shadow? Have you ever met any? I bet you'd like them. Most of them are pretty quiet, and they like to sleep, just like you.

"I miss living with cats sometimes. I wanted to adopt one when I moved here, but it says in my lease that any cats living in the apartment had to be declawed. What an awful rule, right? I bet every other apartment complex got rid of rules like that twenty years ago. Declawing is illegal in a bunch of other countries, you know.

"Anyway, there was no way I was going to have some poor cat mutilated like that just to make my landlord happy, so I decided not to take anyone home for now."

She sighed. "I just love cats, and there are so many out there who need homes, you know? I guess I'll just have to wait though. I love my dogs, too!"

Annie's hand rested on Shadow's back for a moment, and then resumed stroking his fur in a new pattern. Her presence comforted Shadow, although he still refused to look at her.

Annie didn't seem to mind being ignored. She talked to Shadow for hours, one subject flowing into the next. Stories from her childhood. The way her car didn't brake quite right, which was a little worrisome in the snow. The antics of the two dogs who lived with her, Cam and Oliver. Shadow's favorite story of the night was about Cam.

"Cammie's always been a little terrified of the vacuum," Annie said. "He always just goes to hide in the closet whenever I'm cleaning. A few weeks ago though, I was vacuuming behind the couch and the vacuum just stopped all of the sudden. I thought it broke for a moment, but it turned out that the plug just came out of the wall.

"I had it plugged in around the corner in the hallway, so the cord was stretched out pretty far. I just assumed I'd accidentally pulled it out with the vacuum, so I plugged it in and went back to cleaning.

"As soon as I turned the vacuum on though, it shut off again! I ran back around the corner and there was Cam, standing there with the cord in his mouth! He figured out that pulling it out of the wall makes the vacuum stop! I had to teach him to stop doing that of course, but not before I had a good laugh."

Shadow couldn't help but feel a little bit of amusement. He hated the vacuum too, but he hadn't ever thought to pull the plug on it.

As the night went on, Annie rested her head on the blankets only a few feet from Shadow's face. Eventually, she stopped stroking his back and just rested her hand in one place. The stories grew shorter, and the breaks between stories grew longer. In the middle of a story about how she had nearly started a kitchen fire last month, Annie's voice trailed off completely. The steady, rhythmic breathing of sleep took its place.

Only then did Shadow outwardly acknowledge Annie's presence there. He carefully lifted his head and sniffed her the first time, fully taking in her scent. In addition to the human-smell and the dryer lint, Shadow could smell the dogs, Cam and Oliver. The pasta Annie had eaten for dinner lingered on her breath. Whole wheat pasta, with a simple oil and garlic sauce. There was an assortment of vegetables mixed in with the pasta too, but Shadow didn't bother to sort them out. He'd never liked vegetables very much anyway.

Shadow stared at Annie, bewildered. *Who was this woman, who spoke so sweetly and laughed like the birds? And why did she seem to care so much about him?*

A beam of moonlight shone through the kennel's window, illuminating Annie's face. She was young for a human, maybe twenty-four or so. It was always hard to tell with humans. Her hair was the color of wet sand, her skin the color of dry sand. Strands of her hair fell across her face, just barely obscuring her eyes. She slept on her side, with one arm resting on Shadow's back. The other arm was folded under her body, completely hidden except for a slender wrist and a single piece of jewelry: a bent fork. Beyond the fork was Annie's hand, fingers clutching at the drawstrings of her jacket. Shadow had to resist the urge to chew on the drawstrings. Humans didn't seem to appreciate having their clothing chewed on, and he didn't want to upset Annie.

Strange, he thought. *He hadn't wanted to chew anything since Brian left.* Maybe this woman *was* worth liking. Liking her would be alright, he supposed. He had no desire to love her though. He had no desire to ever love a human ever again.

Annie's face suddenly twisted into a scowl. Her fingers tightened around the drawstring, twitching several times before relaxing again. Shadow wondered if she was having a nightmare. Years of living with young children had taught him how to calm a sleeping human without ever waking them, and Shadow employed those skills for Annie. He reached out with a paw, gingerly pushing her forearm down to the blankets. After a brief moment of hesitation, he set his chin down on the paw, careful not to disturb the catheter taped to his forelimb. Annie let out a quiet whimper, but then the muscles in her face slowly relaxed. Within a few heartbeats, all signs of the nightmare were gone.

They stayed like that for the rest of the night, with Annie asleep and Shadow awake. By the end of the night,

Shadow knew Annie perfectly. He knew her by smell, by the sound of her breathing. The touch and tone of her arm, limp and relaxed under his protective paw.

Shadow had never been particularly good at keeping track of the time, but it seemed like morning came earlier than usual that day. When a sunbeam crossed Annie's face, she woke with a start, apparently shocked that she'd fallen asleep. Then she noticed Shadow's paw on her arm and smiled.

"There you go, buddy. I knew there was still someone in there."

Annie gave Shadow a kiss on the top of his head, just as Brian's daughter Bri had done so many times in the past. Then she stood, ran a hand through her disheveled hair, and left Shadow's kennel.

Shadow slept in his corner and ignored the humans for most of the day, still paralyzed by the throbbing ache that had replaced his heartbeat. He couldn't deny that something felt different, though. The aching was certainly still there, painful as ever. But a tiny flicker of warmth had been ignited in Shadow's chest, and it pushed against the cold ache with all of its strength. It faded throughout the day, but came back even stronger ever time Annie visited. She never stayed for the entire night again, but she always managed to keep Shadow company for at least a little while after everyone else had gone home.

On the third night of the visits, Shadow actually raised his head in greeting when Annie entered the kennel. On the fourth, he turned around to face her while she spoke.

Shadow remained dead to the world while the sun was up, but felt himself come to life at night. The warmth in his chest grew every moment he spent with Annie, fighting against the pain with a force and ferocity he didn't know he had. On the fifth night, Shadow found himself resting his head on Annie's lap while she told him about how the heat in her apartment had gone out.

"Of course it had to happen in January," she said. "Last night, I put every blanket I own on my bed. Cam and Ollie stayed under the blankets with me, but it was *still* too cold. I think I'm just going to buy a little space heater for tonight. Knowing my landlord, I'll probably need it for the next week, at least."

Annie stroked the side of Shadow's neck while she talked, and he allowed her touch to comfort him. He only understood some of the stories she told, and was entirely uncertain about what she meant when she talked about things like landlords and leases and space heaters. Despite that little problem, Annie's voice was already on its way to becoming Shadow's favorite sound in the world. She could have talked about anything and he still would have been happy.

Happy. Shadow hadn't ever expected to be happy again.

He pondered the fact that Annie made him feel happy long after she left that night and for most of the next day. He couldn't seem to get her off of his mind, all through the morning and afternoon. *Why was she being so nice to him? Why would a human wear a fork around her wrist? And most of all, when was she coming to see him again?*

When Annie came to tell Shadow a story that night, he actually stood to greet her. She was ecstatic.

"Shadow! You're up!" She knelt down and threw her arms around his neck, but quickly released her grip. "Sorry buddy, I forgot dogs aren't very into hugs."

Annie gave Shadow's back a quick scratch before sitting down by the bed. He followed close behind, settling down onto the blankets and resting his head on her lap. She told a special story that night, about a man she'd met recently. They'd only spoken for a few moments last weekend, but tomorrow they were going to lunch together. His name was Hunter, which wasn't a name she particularly liked, since a boy named Hunter had once teased her on the playground. His personality made up for it though, and his looks, too. Annie giggled about that last comment before listing off his features—a strong jaw, neat blonde hair, icy blue eyes, and a mischievous grin. She wanted their date to go well, and she confessed that she was incredibly nervous.

Shadow realized that Annie must trust him, to open up about her secrets like that. It was the same thing his old family had once done. The children would come home from school and tell him about their bad day, or Amy would explain that she didn't get the promotion, or Brian would confide in Shadow about a recent quarrel with his wife. Shadow knew everyone's secrets, probably because he listened to everyone so well. And when he learned a secret, it was safe with him.

Annie finished her story by telling Shadow she wished summer would arrive, so tomorrow's date could be outside instead of indoors.

"I love being outside. I just feel so cooped up in the winter, you know? All I want is a nice day in the park, surrounded by trees and fresh air. With enough clouds to keep things cool, but not so many that it gets dark. I like to go for jogs in the park during the summer, you know. There's nothing quite like the way the wind feels on your face, especially when you get going fast."

Shadow's tail wagged a little as he pictured Annie's day in the park. He loved feeling the wind on his face too, even if he wasn't able to run particularly fast anymore. However, he had to disagree about feeling cooped up in the winter. Plowing through deep snow was Shadow's favorite outdoor activity.

Annie glanced at Shadow's wagging tail and smiled. Her voice took on an excited tone. "Do you like going outside, buddy?"

Shadow allowed his tongue to loll out of his mouth in affirmation. He didn't even mind that Annie had called him buddy.

"Well," said Annie, "you be good and start eating your food and getting up for walks, okay? Then you can go outside! I'll take you myself!"

Shadow decided he liked that idea, and allowed his tail to wag a little more. Annie smiled and rose to leave, giving his side a gentle pat. "You're getting better, buddy. I'm proud of you.

"Good night, Shadow." Annie stepped through the kennel's gate and shut it behind her. Then she swept her gaze across the rest of the kennels and said, "Good night puppies!"

Shadow watched Annie leave, and for a long time after the door's hinges creaked shut, he didn't move. He'd broken his vow to never get up, but something about Annie made him want to be a dog again, all full of life and energy.

For the first time in over a week, Shadow realized how hungry and thirsty he was. He walked—or limped, since refusing to move for a week is particularly hard on old joints— to his food and water bowls and set himself the task of regaining his strength.

Chapter 6

The next morning, Shadow sat facing the front of his kennel. The day took on a different tone with the new view, and it greatly helped his mood. Early in the morning, an army of humans Shadow had previously ignored refilled each dog's food and water. Excited barking echoed down the hall, quieted only by the ring of dry food landing in hard bowls. The humans were delighted to see that Shadow's bowl was empty, so they gave him an extra scoop. He appreciated the gesture, although he wished they would just bring some less crumbly food.

A short time later, the same army returned with mops. This concerned Shadow at first, but after a while, he realized that the mops meant no harm and only wanted to wash away any excrement left in the kennels overnight. Throughout the morning, everyone who entered Shadow's kennel was sure to give him a few quick scratches or a pat on the back, explaining to him how glad they were that he was finally up. He accepted their kindness, but didn't reciprocate. His affection was still reserved for Annie. She had *earned* it.

Annie arrived around midday with another woman, who Shadow identified as the owner of the voice that urged him to get up for walks. She had close-cropped black hair, dotted with little silver flecks that glinted like stars in a midnight sky. Her skin was a rich brown at least two shades darker than Shadow's eyes. She seemed surprised that Shadow was actually up, but clipped a leash to his collar without questioning it.

"Hey, buddy!" Annie exclaimed. "I'm so glad you're up this morning. I hear you've been eating and drinking too!

"This is Kim," she said, motioning to the woman. "She's been coming to take you on walks recently, but I told her I'd take you today."

Annie was such a thoughtful human, always taking the time to explain things to Shadow. He liked knowing what was going on, and being in on the plan made him trust Annie even more.

Kim passed the leash to Annie and reached down to stroke Shadow's fur. Since the air was still full of the floor cleaner's harsh smell, Shadow had trouble picking out her scent until she was already touching him. Mostly, Kim smelled like children—two of them—and the sticky syrup one of them had undoubtedly spilled on her hand that morning. Most of the syrup had been washed away, but Shadow licked at Kim's hand just in case there was any left.

"Oh, so now you like me, huh? Are you going to cooperate today, Shadow?" Kim laughed and turned to Annie. "Of course, on the day *I'm* not taking him out."

Annie held up her hands in feigned offense. "Hey, I spent a lot of time gaining his trust! I think he's just been really upset about being left here. Anthony told me the guy who dropped him off had him for eleven years, and then just ditched him."

"Yeah," said Kim. "I heard that too. Poor guy. Well, anyway, I'm glad he's finally up." She gave Shadow's head one last pat, then stood and opened the kennel's gate.

Annie followed Kim through the open gate, motioning for Shadow to follow. "Come on buddy! Let's go for a walk!"

Shadow followed Annie down the hall and through several sets of doors. When they finally went through a door that led outside, a gust of cold air whipped through Shadow's fur. He stared at the gray clouds overhead, dark against the steam curling up from his nostrils. Shadow had always been amused by the way his breath turned to steam in the cold. He had always tried to bite the steam when he was a puppy, back before he learned it couldn't be caught.

After Annie zipped up her coat, they set off toward the trail behind the shelter. Annie let Shadow choose the pace, which made his stiff joints quite grateful. After so much time lying down, walking around felt absolutely wonderful. *Walking with Annie was much better than lying in a corner all day,* Shadow decided.

It was an easy trail—the wide, flat kind made for bikes—and nowhere near as challenging as the trails Shadow had once conquered with Brian. Still, he tired quickly. After only a few hundred yards, it was time to turn back. Shadow stopped and stared up at Annie, who immediately understood.

"Tired, buddy?"

Shadow turned and led Annie back to the shelter. Once he was in his kennel again, she unclipped the leash from his collar, called him a good boy, scratched his head, and went off to perform her other chores for the day.

Good boy. The warmth in Shadow's chest swelled, pushing the cold ache out a little more. He was glad Annie had taken him for a walk. He wished he could have gone farther, but his joints were beyond stiff, and refusing food for so long can certainly detract from a dog's ability to walk. Short as it was, the walk still made Shadow hungry. He took a few crumbly bites from his bowl, and then settled down on his bed to watch the people in the hallway. All kinds of unfamiliar humans came and went, but it wasn't until a child and his father stopped by Shadow's kennel that he realized not everyone was a worker. *This family wanted to take him home!* Excitement bubbled up in Shadow's stomach, but thinking of home quickly brought on memories of the family he'd lost. Almost instantly, the excitement fizzled out again.

The child pointed and tugged on his father's pants, but Shadow turned away. The wounds left on his heart by one family were still too fresh to start looking for another. Shadow ignored everyone who came by for the rest of the day, but he made sure to eat and drink again once the shelter closed. For Annie, if not for himself.

As the days went by, Shadow got stronger. The idea of looking for a new family became less painful, and he even ventured to let potential adopters pat his head or give him a few scratches behind the ears. He ate his crumbly food every day, and managed to make friends with the dog from across the hall when they were in the common room together. She had a strange way of biting his ankles when she wanted to play, but never with her full strength. Shadow always humored the smaller dog, but never let his teeth touch her for fear that the difference in their sizes would actually cause her harm.

Annie's after-hours visits became a rarity, and Shadow found that he missed their talks. The stronger he got though, the longer their walks—and Annie's stories—could be. Words poured out of her, though she only seemed willing to tell the best stories when there weren't other humans around to hear. Since humans had such a pitiful hearing range, that wasn't much of a problem.

On one walk, she said that her apartment's heat had finally been fixed, but only after she'd pestered her landlord for two weeks. She also mentioned that she had a second date with Hunter, and proceeded to talk about him for a very long time. Shadow didn't care much about Hunter, but Annie's excitement about the date was contagious. His tail wagged whenever she brought it up.

"I was a little worried after the first date," said Annie, "because he picked out a steakhouse, and then he seemed kind of annoyed when he found out I don't eat meat. But I was like, "sorry dude." I loved animals *way* before I met you. I'm not gonna eat one just for your sake. He ended up being flexible about it though, and when we went to a Thai place instead, he was respectful enough to order a meal without any meat. And then he called me for another date last night, so I guess I was all worried over nothing!"

During another walk, Annie explained how Ollie had once managed to hide for a full two hours to avoid a trip to the vet. By the time she finally found him cowering in a cabinet under the kitchen sink, the vet had closed for the day.

What a great way to avoid the vet, Shadow thought. He didn't mind the vet much anymore, but wished *he'd* thought of that as a puppy.

On the days after storms, Annie complained about the snow. Shadow respectfully listened, but he couldn't have disagreed more. In fact, he spent every snowy walk finding the deepest possible powder to sink his paws into.

On a day when the snow was particularly deep, Shadow got the chance to do one of his favorite things: plowing through snow with his chest. Crouching in the deepest part, he pushed forward until the snow packed together and stopped him from going any farther. He sampled a few bites of snow while he caught his breath, but ultimately decided it wasn't the right kind for eating. Too heavy. He moved on after another moment, climbing over the packed snow and plowing a brand new path. Icy slush built up in his collar, but he didn't mind. Playing in the snow was much too fun to worry about a little thing like the cold.

Shadow gave Annie his open-mouthed smile and barked out an invitation for her to come join him. She stuck to the path though, folding her arms over the leash and shaking her head. Apparently, she felt the need to act disappointed that he'd gotten himself so covered in snow. Her grin gave her away though, and before long, she was laughing.

When they returned from the walk, Shadow found his kennel full of fresh blankets and harsh cleaner smell. He wrinkled his nose at the scent, but had to admit it was better than a dirty kennel.

Annie unclipped Shadow's leash, and then spent several minutes smoothing out the fur on his back. "You're going to find such a good family, buddy. I just know it."

She told him that every day. She always told him he was a good boy, too, and Annie's praises made Shadow happier than anything else. He adored this human, and it seemed like she adored him back. The warmth in his heart grew a little more, despite the freezing slush trapped beneath his collar. No cold lasted long against the warmth felt by a happy dog. Not even slush. Not even the fading ache in Shadow's heart.

Chapter 7

"ADOPT A SENIOR DOG DAY!"

A sign in the common room displayed those five words in cheerful, brightly colored letters. Shadow couldn't read, of course, but Annie had explained the sign to him that morning. He supposed that the term "senior dog" referred to him, though he wasn't exactly certain what a senior was. Annie had asked him to be on his best behavior, and told him she had a good feeling that he was going home today. Shadow hoped she was right. He'd lost track of how long he'd been at the shelter, but it seemed like forever.

Annie left him in the common room with three other dogs, Kim, and a round-faced man Shadow recognized but couldn't name. Kim and the man stood in the adoption office adjacent to the common room, watching the dogs through a window in the wall and making sure to enter the room when any potential adopters came in.

Of the dogs at the adoption event, only one looked older than Shadow. Arthritis had ravaged her joints, and her face twisted in pain every time she walked. Next to her, another dog—the smallest dog in the room—seemed almost out of place. The little dog had some gray around her nose, but behaved almost like a puppy. The oldest dog didn't even bother trying to play with her, but Shadow and a Border Collie gave it their best effort. The Collie lasted much longer than Shadow did.

The first potential adopter to enter the room was a middle-aged woman, taller than most of the other humans Shadow had met. She asked about each of the dogs, and Shadow carefully listened while Kim read information from an adoption sheet. The oldest dog was a shepherd mix named Riley, and Shadow had been right about her age. She was fourteen, and had apparently been doing very well before the arthritis took over. Now she could only go for short walks, and stairs were close to impossible, so she either needed a home without stairs or a human willing to carry her. She'd been at the shelter for nearly six months. Shadow detected a faintly urgent undertone in Kim's voice when she read that part, but he wasn't sure why.

The little dog was only nine, which offered some explanation for her good health. She was a terrier, her name was Ruby, and she'd only been at the shelter for a week. The Border Collie was a purebred, creatively named Callie. She was ten, and had spent exactly four weeks at the shelter.

Kim paused when she got to Shadow, glancing up and down the adoption sheet. "This is Shadow…" She turned to the round-faced man. "Hey James, I don't think we know Shadow's breed."

James laughed. "Call him a shepherd mix. That's what I always do when I don't know."

"Alright," Kim said. "Well, Shadow's twelve and he's been with us for about six weeks now. He was really upset when he first got here, but he's really come a long way. I think he'll improve even more with some extra love."

The woman politely spent a few moments with each dog, but it was over as soon as she got to Ruby. Kim led her into the adoption office after only a short time, and the two set to work filling out the necessary forms. Shadow could hear their words through the glass, though he didn't give the conversation too much thought.

"What's your full name?" asked Kim.

"Linda Ashwood," said the woman.

"What type of residence do you live in?"

"I own a home. We have a yard, with a fence."

"Will the dog live inside with you or out in the yard?"

"Inside, of course."

"Good. Do you live with anyone else, and are they aware that you're here adopting Ruby today?"

"Just my husband and yes, he knows."

"Alright," Kim said. "I'm going to let you fill out the rest of this form yourself while I call a reference. Could I please have a name and phone number for your reference?"

Linda Ashwood gave Kim a reference and filled out the form. As soon as the reference check came out clean, Ruby's adoption fee was paid and she went home.

People came and went throughout the rest of the day, ushered in by the shelter staff. A few seemed genuinely interested, but most just listened politely before asking if there were any puppies available, or quietly stating that they had come for "a younger, more energetic dog."

Despite his insistence, Kim managed to change the mind of one man who wanted a puppy. "Senior dogs tend to already be trained," she said. "All of these dogs certainly are. And they're calm. Way past their destructive puppy phases."

The man knelt down in the center of the room, but seemed far from convinced. "That would be nice, but I do worry about—oh, hi there!" He laughed as Callie sniffed at the back of his neck. The Collie gave the man a few quick licks, and then rested her chin on his shoulder.

Kim smiled. "Older dogs still have plenty of love to give, too. That's Callie. She *loves* chin scratches."

"Is that true, Callie?" the man asked. He rubbed the side of Callie's chin, and she panted in appreciation. It only took a few more minutes of chin scratching and face licking before Callie had a home, which left only Shadow and Riley.

Shadow settled down to the floor, patiently waiting for more visitors. Riley didn't seem to have much interest in playing, but she did hobble over to Shadow's side. Every time the older dog took a step, she put her paw down again as quickly as possible to ease the pressure in her joints. Shadow recognized the technique, since he'd been experimenting with it himself. It wasn't as effective as he had hoped, but it seemed to work better for him than it did for Riley.

Riley slumped down next to Shadow, and each of them took a moment to sniff the other. Shadow could certainly smell Riley's age. Not that age itself had a smell, but there were clues. A dusty scent that came from spending more time lying down than standing up. A distinct lack of the scents of fear and hostility, signaling the sort of calm confidence only a fourteen-year-old dog could have. Riley's gentle, quiet presence put Shadow at ease, and he was grateful for the company.

Aside from Kim and James, Riley was the only company who stuck around very long. Visitors came and went throughout the afternoon, but they were always friendly enough. They'd pat Riley's head or scratch Shadow's back, and quite a few of them remarked about how cute it was that the two dogs were lying side by side. Shadow made sure to lick the faces of the humans he liked, which ended up being all of them. They claimed to like him too, but they always left in the end, and none of them seemed interested in taking Shadow or Riley home.

As the hours crept by, Kim and James devised clever plans to show off the dogs' good behavior. At one point, Kim even left a couple of treats on the ground. Just as the dogs stood to eat, Kim commanded them to leave the food alone.

"Leave it... leave it." To Shadow's left, Riley whined. His own muscles twitched in anticipation, and he struggled to hold himself back. The treats were so close he could smell them, and treats were meant to be eaten.

Finally, Kim relented. "Go!" she shouted. The treats were gone in seconds.

People applauded the trick, but it apparently wasn't enough. Excuses were offered up, and by late afternoon Shadow had lost track of how many people "were looking for a dog who was a little younger." Eventually, the adoption event had to end, and Kim and James set to work cleaning up the common room.

"Well," said Kim as she unpinned the banner from the wall, "I guess two isn't too bad. I wish we'd been able to find homes for all four of them though."

"I know," said James. "I know she still has plenty of time, but I'm starting to worry about Riley. She's already halfway through her year."

"She's so sweet," said Kim. "I don't want to see her get put down. I mean I know we have to turn those kennels over eventually, but they should make exceptions for sweet old dogs like Riley."

She paused, then added, "Shadow too. He's come so far. He even lets me walk him now. I don't know what Annie did, but she breathed life back into that dog. He loves her. I just can't stand the idea of any of those sweet dogs ending up—"

James made a sound somewhere between a laugh and a grunt. "Don't worry about Shadow quite yet. He still has almost eleven months. They'll both make it. Almost everyone does.

"And they're much better off here than the Bluff County Shelter. Dogs only get a few weeks over there. A year is longer than almost any other shelter I've heard of. I'm actually surprised Anthony got the board to push it out anywhere close to that far."

James thought for a moment, then said, "But don't get me wrong, I care about them too. I just think they'll be alright. Don't worry.

"Don't worry," James said again, this time addressing Shadow and Riley. "You two will both find good homes."

He knelt down to pet the dogs, and Shadow's tail swished excitedly through the air. He decided Kim and James could both be counted as friends, and Riley too. The new friends made him happy, but he still couldn't manage to shake the disappointment that no one had taken him home. Not for the first time, Shadow wondered if there was something wrong with him. *Why else wouldn't anyone want to take him home? Why else had he been left behind in the first place?*

Chapter 8

Shadow liked getting scratches almost anywhere, but his favorite spot was rather specific: on the side of his neck, ranging from behind his ears to the base of his jaw. Whenever someone scratched Shadow there, his hind leg thumped the floor. Sometimes, his tail even wagged so hard it threatened to knock breakables off of tables, when breakables and tables were around.

And this man had discovered Shadow's favorite spot in less than a minute. Impressive, considering that some of the volunteers still hadn't figured it out in the three months he'd been at the shelter. Shadow immediately decided he liked the man.

He was a young man, with black glasses and a head of curly black hair. The hairs on his fingers were almost as curly as the hair on his head, but the *really* important thing about his fingers was how good they were at giving scratches. The man and his fiancée were looking to adopt a dog together, and Kim thought Shadow would be a perfect match. Shadow had come to trust Kim's judgement on matters like that, since she spent more time with him than anyone besides Annie. She always took excellent care of him on Annie's days off, one of which was today.

The man knelt in front of Shadow and turned to Kim. "You know, he actually looks like he's in pretty good shape for being twelve."

His fingers scratched the perfect spot at that moment, and Shadow's tail thumped out a beat on the floor.

Kim smiled. "I think he likes you. I bet he'd love to go home with you."

To emphasize this point, Shadow launched a series of licks at the man's face. The man laughed and tried to push Shadow away, but seemed willing to tolerate at least a few licks. *Perfect.*

"I like him too," the man said, wiping off his smeared glasses. "And he has such a pretty coat. Like a penny.

"We really had a puppy in mind, but this guy is awesome. I'm going to talk to my fiancée tonight and see what she thinks. Maybe I'll bring her to meet him next weekend."

Excitement bubbled up in Shadow's chest. This man seemed like a wonderful person to go home with, and he was more than ready to get out of the shelter. Three long months spent in a kennel can certainly wear on a dog, and Shadow's joints ached from the lack of motion. Boredom was a problem too. It plagued him almost every day, although daily walks and the occasional visit from Annie helped. He'd gotten a new ball recently too, and that offered some entertainment. Still, the shelter wasn't home. Shadow wanted to go *home.*

"We'll leave you a number so you can call about him once you make a decision," said Kim. "What did you say your name was?"

"Adam."

"Well Adam, I think you and Shadow would be wonderful together."

Kim led Adam out of the kennel and closed the door behind them. Just before they disappeared through the door at the end of the hallway, Adam smiled back at Shadow and gave him a wave.

To Shadow, that wave was as good as a belly rub. It meant friendship. A promise to return. *A new family.* Warmth spread throughout his entire body, suddenly even *better* than a belly rub. *Home.* He was finally going home!

Shadow snatched up the new ball on his way back to the bed and chewed gleefully for the rest of the afternoon. The tennis ball, as Annie called it, had recently been added to Shadow's kennel in addition to the plastic toy he'd been chewing on for the last few months. The ball was better than the old toy in almost every way. It took Shadow some time to fit it into his mouth, but the reward was worth the effort when he finally did. Every time he clamped down, the ball pushed back, almost like it wanted to play with him. *Bite down, spring back.*

Shadow settled into a delightful rhythm with the ball, working his jaws all around it until the fuzzy surface was completely matted with saliva. *Bite down, spring back. Bite down, spring back.*

A soft bark made Shadow look up. The dog with messy brown fur had gone home, so a new dog had taken up residence in the kennel across the hall. The new dog—a lab with pale yellow fur—gave Shadow a soft whine, apparently wanting to play with the ball.

Shadow was more than willing to share, especially with younger dogs. After all, a young dog had a much greater need for chewing than an old dog did. However, two chain link gates stood between them, and not even a tennis ball would fit through those. Shadow dropped the ball and rested a paw on it in case it tried to bounce away. Then he gave the lab a sympathetic whine, unsure of what else to do. *Maybe he could sneak the ball into the common room someday. Then they could play together, and this new dog would become his friend!*

The lab stared at the ball and bit at the gate that held him back. He whined and paced the floor, but gave up after only a few minutes and fell asleep on the hard concrete. This amused Shadow. *Why would the lab choose to sleep on concrete when he could choose to sleep on a significantly softer bed?*

Seeing the lab sleep made Shadow realize he was tired too, so he carried the tennis ball over to the bed. He decided to hide his face beneath a blanket, since the sun's angle made the kennel too bright to sleep comfortably. Arranging the blanket wasn't an easy task. Shadow had to push his nose under the tangled fabric and lift it into the air, then race to stick his face beneath it before it fell back to the bed. That last bit was the hard part.

The blanket fell in a silent heap just in front of Shadow's nose, which did nothing to block the light. He snorted at the blanket's defiance, then tossed it back into the air. In the past, any humans who caught Shadow digging his way under a blanket had always made a scene, loudly cooing about "how cute" he was. Fortunately, his third attempt was successful and he plopped onto the bed before any humans noticed. The tennis ball slipped out of his mouth and bounced across the kennel, but he was already too sleepy to retrieve it. Warm air quickly filled the space beneath the blanket, and thoughts of going home with Adam filled Shadow's mind. Sleep came within a matter of minutes.

The dissonant barks that normally echoed down the hall were unusually quiet, so Shadow slept soundly all afternoon. Long after closing time though, his ears registered the telltale click of the latch on the hallway door. Down the hall, barking dogs rushed to the front of their kennels to confirm the presence of a visitor. Shadow rushed to the front of his kennel too, hoping to see Annie. *Who else could it be?* None of the other workers ever came back as late as she did.

He heard Annie long before he saw or smelled her. He'd memorized the sound her feet made on the concrete floor; the gentle clack of the fork on her wrist hitting the doorknob; the fruitless shushing of the barking dogs as she made her way down the hall.

Annie greeted Shadow with a whispered "Hey buddy!" and stepped into the kennel. Shadow would have jumped for joy, if jumping didn't hurt his knees. Instead, he settled for dancing around in place and sniffing Annie's hands.

"Want your ball?"

In the dark, Annie's nimble hands placed the tennis ball right under Shadow's nose. He gladly accepted it, and then went back to sniffing. Annie smelled of lilac soap and the man, Hunter. *And food!* Shadow's nose led him straight to the scent's source, which came from the pocket of Annie's jacket. As soon as he was certain about the food's location, he let the ball drop with a dull thud. Shadow sniffed again, prodding Annie's pocket until she laughed and gave his face a gentle push.

"Hold on, hold on!" Annie took an eternity to sit next to Shadow's bed, and another eternity to unzip her pocket. When she finally reached inside, she produced exactly what he'd been waiting for: a small paper bag, containing slightly less than half of a breadstick.

Shadow sat down so fast it hurt his butt. Sitting in the presence of human food was a reflex, developed from a lifetime of begging for a bite. *He hadn't eaten human food in months!*

"Yep, just for you!" Annie said. "Shhh. Don't tell the other dogs. I don't think I'm allowed to give you this."

She tossed the breadstick to Shadow, and he snapped it out of the air immediately. It was gone within seconds, leaving traces of its salty, flaky goodness all over his mouth.

Annie laughed. "Hey," she teased, "that's the fastest I've ever seen you move."

She patiently waited for Shadow to hunt down any crumbs that had escaped to the floor. When he finished and plopped down on the bed, she scratched the back of his head.

"I'm so glad to see you buddy! Hunter lives just off of Oak, so the shelter's right on the way home from his place. I thought I'd stop by and see you since I haven't been here in a few days! How are you doing?"

Shadow wanted to tell Annie how bored he was, but couldn't think of a good way to put it into terms a human would understand.

"I bet it gets pretty boring in here, huh?" said Annie.

Shadow licked her face. Somehow, Annie always understood. It was one of the many things he loved about her.

"Don't worry, soon the weather will warm up and you can go hang out in the dog run! Then you'll get to be outside for longer. And you'll get to be around the other puppies more!" Annie had a way of calling dogs puppies no matter how old they were.

"Are you excited for spring, Shadow? I tell ya' buddy, this snow stuff isn't for me. I don't like driving in it, or walking in it. And if my hands get too cold, my fingers turn all white, starting right here at the second knuckle. Then it takes *forever* for me to be able to even feel them again. I guess I should move somewhere warmer. Someday when I'm rich, right?"

Shadow couldn't understand why Annie complained about something as fun as snow so much. He loved the little things she told him though, so he listened anyway.

"I have tomorrow off too and I'm going to spend it with Hunter, but I'll be back on Tuesday! I got lucky and landed three days in a row off this week, so I've been spending lots of time with Ollie and Cam and Hunter. I wish you could meet them. I think you'd like them all."

She paused and looked at Shadow. "How silly of me! I've never told you that much about any of them besides Hunter, have I?"

Shadow wagged his tail, eager to hear more about Cam and Oliver. Annie was so thoughtful, always sure to keep him in the loop. Every other human talked to him like a dog, but Annie talked to him like she was talking to another human. Never mind that he didn't understand half of what she said. He loved her for it anyway.

"Both Cam and Ollie came from here. Oliver's five, but he still has a lot of puppy energy. If it's still light out when I get home, I usually try to run him so he doesn't chew up my stuff. He sleeps in bed with me, and always burrows through the blankets down to the very bottom of the bed."

She laughed. "Then he farts all night and I have to hold my breath when I get up in the morning!

"Cam's a little older. He's actually a lot like you. He's patient with Ollie and he's starting to slow down a little bit, but he's a happy guy. I don't know what kind of dog he is, but he's *big*. And of course he always wants to sit on my lap. Big dogs always seem to want to do that."

Annie laughed. Then she sighed and said, "I wish I could take you home to live with us, buddy. My landlord limits me to two dogs, which is actually the most I've been able to find in any apartment around here. She's so strict about it though, and she's so suspicious of me. Always doing random property inspections to make sure 'my dogs didn't wreck anything.' "

"But you know what, buddy? I'm going to talk to her about it anyway. Maybe she'll make an exception for you, since you're so well-behaved. In the meantime, we'll keep looking to find you a home!"

Shadow gave Annie that open-mouthed smile, which lasted long after the conversation shifted away from homes and to the man, Hunter. He seemed to find a place in nearly every conversation, but Shadow didn't mind. Annie's perpetual smile somehow grew even wider when Hunter came up, and if she was happy, Shadow was happy.

"Your breadstick came from Nonna's—that's where Hunter took me for dinner tonight. It's this little Italian place just off of Cherry Street. It was *so* good. I was so excited when I found out that the breadsticks were just glazed with oil instead of butter, I think I ate a whole basket! But I made sure to save a little for you!

"After dinner we went to his house and watched *Empty Whisper*. Have you ever seen that one? I didn't like it much to be honest. Everyone said it was great, but I guess I'm just not into horror movies. I can't even watch them unless I'm with Hunter.

"Tomorrow we aren't going out. Probably just a few drinks at his house. I'll let you know how it goes!" Annie paused. "Hey, Hunter's pretty good with Cam and Ollie…

Maybe he could take you home! That would be cool, right? Then we'd all get to be together.

"You know what? I'll talk to him tomorrow, for sure! I'd be the happiest girl in the world if he gave you a home, and I don't see a reason why he couldn't. I know you haven't met him, but don't worry, I'll scope 'im out and report back!"

She gave Shadow a mock salute and stood to leave. He followed her to the kennel's gate, and she smiled. "I should probably get home to Cam and Ollie, but I'll see you on Tuesday, alright buddy?"

Shadow licked Annie's hand, and she bent down to kiss the top of his head. Then she stepped out of the kennel and disappeared down the hallway, shushing the few barking dogs who were still awake. Shadow watched her go, and then returned to his bed still wearing that open-mouthed smile. Annie's visits always left him with plenty of questions, such as where Cherry Street was, but there was no question about why she made him smile. She made his heart feel warm, and going to bed with a warm heart always made for the best nights.

Bit by bit, Shadow was breaking his vow to never love a human again. He knew it was happening, but had given up on fighting it. He had tried to hold out over the months, but he was only a dog, and a dog's heart is made to love. How could he *not* love a human who cared for him so much?

With the realization that he loved Annie came the realization that he still loved his old family too. That hurt, but the pain seemed to disappear whenever Annie was around. Perhaps it was time to stop letting his old family keep him from being happy.

For the rest of the night, Shadow couldn't help but think about going for a walk with Annie on Tuesday. And then there was the idea of meeting this man she talked about so much. *Two possible homes, all in the same day.*

His tail didn't stop wagging until the moment he fell asleep.

Chapter 9

As promised, Annie took Shadow for a walk when Tuesday came. Spring had arrived in full force, and the smells of a hundred plants and animals coming out of their winter slumber assaulted Shadow's nostrils.

By the time they reached the trail behind the shelter, some of the smells were so strong that Shadow could *taste* them. Fresh grass. The faint scent of a few baby leaves budding on otherwise bare trees. Squirrels, hiding somewhere deep in the forest off to the left. The recently returned birds, who added sounds to the smells.

He drank it all in, smiling up at Annie the entire time.

"Isn't this wonderful?" she asked.

Shadow had to agree that it *was* wonderful. He loved the snow, but somehow he always forgot about the explosion of life that came with each spring. The once-tranquil world was suddenly full of sound, and every creature had their own song to sing. An entire orchestra waited in the woods near the path, warming up for summer's grand presentation. Even if spring meant the inevitable disappearance of snow, it was certainly wonderful in its own way.

Annie allowed Shadow to absorb spring's sudden arrival for a while, but she couldn't stay quiet for long. Shadow suspected she loved their talks as much as he did.

"I heard someone came in last weekend, buddy. I heard he might adopt you! You didn't tell me that!"

Shadow's only response was panting at Annie with that open-mouthed smile.

"I knew you'd get to go home soon. You're such a good boy."

A couple of birds darted across the path, chasing each other into the trees. Shadow and Annie watched them disappear, and then resumed walking in silence. When Annie spoke again, her voice sounded subdued. *Or had it been subdued before?* Shadow had been too enthralled by spring to notice, but he suddenly realized Annie's entire mood had been subdued all day. She clearly needed to get something off her chest.

"Hunter and I had our first big fight last night. We've had little disagreements before, and I guess I knew a big one was coming sometime. It's normal to argue every once and a while, I guess. He did something that really bothered me though."

They paused at the usual turning point and headed back toward the shelter. Shadow anxiously stared up at Annie, still panting but no longer smiling. Something was wrong. He could hear it in her voice.

"We got into shouting a little bit, which I guess isn't so bad. I was shouting too. But at one point, he reached out and swiped a lamp off of a side table. Just smacked it to the ground, and the whole thing shattered. It really scared me.

"I don't know why it bothered me so much. I guess people who express their anger by breaking things just seem... out of control to me, you know? I called a cab and left right away. I didn't even wait for it inside, just stood on the curb. At least it was warm last night."

Annie thought for a moment and added, "I don't know buddy, maybe I'm just overreacting. He's never done anything like that before. We both had a little more to drink than usual last night, so I wonder if that was part of it. He called this morning and apologized, so I think everything's probably alright.

"Oh and I um... didn't get a chance to talk to him about taking you home because of what happened. I think maybe I'll wait a little bit on that."

Annie held the shelter's door open and led Shadow through the series of hallways back to his kennel. After taking off his leash, she made sure to give him a few good scratches.

"You're such a good listener," she said. "Thanks buddy."

Annie left to take other dogs for walks, but came back later to show Shadow the dog run. She explained that the weather was nice today, so they were going to open it up, but that Shadow shouldn't get too used to it because there were probably still a few cold days left in the year.

The dog run turned out to be a large, fenced-in area on the shelter's west side. Shadow loved it from the moment he set foot in it. Overhead was open sky, and he could hear and smell all that the nearby forest had to offer. A bird flitted by overhead, yielding a series of barks from a pair of younger dogs in the center of the run.

Even better than the dog run itself was the fact that Riley was already waiting near the fence. She had positioned herself far from the noise and antics of the other dogs, and Shadow admired her wisdom. He never would have thought of that, and probably would have ended up with a ball or paw in the face.

Shadow retrieved a toy—some long, hard thing made for chewing—and plopped down next to Riley. He positioned the toy so he could chew on half, leaving the other half available for Riley. She quickly got the message, and they happily gnawed together until Riley fell asleep. Shadow waited quietly while she slept, deciding he'd rather enjoy the time outside than waste it by sleeping. The sun warmed his fur, and Riley's gentle breathing added to the symphony of sounds coming from the nearby woods. It was a perfect day, and Shadow felt better than he had in months. He even briefly considered joining the dogs chasing each other across the run, but ultimately decided he was happier just watching. It was enough to simply imagine running that fast again.

Shadow stayed by Riley's side all afternoon, until the sun dropped low and Kim came to take them back inside. He missed the dog run as soon as they left, and hoped he'd be able to return soon.

He did return, twice more that week. Each time, Shadow trotted straight to the sunspot, where Riley was already waiting. They stayed there all afternoon, basking in the gentle spring sun together. There was no need to chase each other around like the younger dogs; each one's presence was enough for the other.

That weekend, Adam returned with his fiancée and they took Shadow to the dog run to play. Shadow could hardly contain himself, and his tail wagged so hard he could barely keep his feet beneath him. Annie decided to let Riley out too, and for a brief moment, Shadow felt like a puppy again. The sunshine, a future family, Riley, and Annie, all together in the dog run. It was almost too much to handle.

Adam's fiancée, a woman named Sarah, turned out to be quite friendly. Shadow made sure to spend plenty of time with both her and Adam, even putting in the effort of retrieving a ball they threw. He didn't exactly run for the ball—anything more than a trot hurt too much—but fetch was a game Shadow knew well. He made a beeline for the ball every time one of the humans threw it, then marched straight back to deposit it in a waiting hand. After the game of fetch was over, Shadow showered Adam and Sarah with kisses, leaving drool all over Adam's glasses again. He made the humans laugh at every possible opportunity, and nearly exploded with excitement when Adam showed Sarah his favorite spot to be scratched.

Annie did her best to get Shadow adopted too, making sure to mention all of his best traits to the young couple. She did it in a casual sort of way, saying little things like, "Last week I took him on a walk, and he knew the exact route all by himself. He's such a smart guy." Or, "That dog over there is his friend Riley. Shadow seems to be able to make friends with just about anyone, but Riley's his best friend. She's an older dog too. Senior dogs tend to be pretty well-behaved, you know. Shadow only chews on things he's supposed to chew on, and he's usually very quiet. He seems to want to be friends with every dog here. And the humans too!"

To emphasize Annie's last point, Shadow flopped down in front of Sarah and rolled onto his back for a belly rub. She obliged, and he squirmed with delight. It got even better when Annie knelt down to help and smiled at Sarah. "The way he's showing you his belly like that? That means he trusts you."

Adam and Sarah stayed for quite a while, but they eventually left with promises that they'd talk about it. Shadow was a little disappointed that they didn't take him home, but Annie explained that Adam promised he'd be back the next weekend.

Satisfied, Shadow settled down next to Riley and rested his head on her outstretched paw. Riley's warmth chased away any discomfort Shadow felt about not going home, and her steady breathing quickly lulled him to sleep. Trying to get adopted was hard work, and he was worn out.

Chapter 10

Shadow wished he could close his ears the way he closed his eyes. He hadn't ever seen the puppies who lived at the far end of the hall, but he certainly heard them. They barked at every human who came by their kennels, which meant they barked a lot.

According to Annie, puppies were easy to adopt out, but adult dogs were a little harder. Because of this, the hallway was arranged so that adult dogs were closer to the door and puppies lived down at the very end. That way, anyone looking for a puppy would see the older dogs first and consider taking one home. It had all made sense when Annie explained it, but Shadow still didn't understand what made so much barking necessary.

Kim claimed that Adam was coming back soon, and Shadow hoped she was right. The peace and quiet of a new home couldn't come soon enough. The puppies *were* all the way at the end of the hall, but the squeaky, grating quality of their voices more than made up for the distance.

Shadow considered silencing the puppies with the loud, superior bark that comes only from years of practice, but decided against it. They would probably just bark back, anyway. Instead, he sighed and paced back and forth by the kennel's gate. He wasn't going to waste a single second once Adam arrived.

Relief washed over Shadow when Adam finally entered the hallway. *Kim had been right!* He resisted the urge to bark, but he did press his face against the kennel's door to get a better look at his new human. *Home! It was time to go home!* Shadow's tail wagged so fiercely that it moved his entire body. Adam smiled and waved, but he didn't stop. Instead, he walked right past Shadow's kennel and *kept going down the hall.*

Shadow let out a soft whine as Adam disappeared from view, but forced himself to be patient. There was nothing to worry about. Adam would return, fill out the necessary forms, and take Shadow off to his new home. *That was how it was supposed to work.*

While he waited for Adam to return, Shadow occupied himself with what had become his favorite pastime: imagining his new life with Adam and Sarah. He pictured himself napping in warm sunspots in their house (or what he imagined their house to be like), or stretched across the couch with them while they watched a movie he had no interest in. Slow, gentle walks. A much bigger space than a kennel, with no barking puppies down the hall. Soft, carpeted floors instead of concrete. And of course, plenty of scratches in his favorite spot

Maybe they would even have a backyard, and Sarah would throw a ball for Shadow while Adam watched. Fetch was more tiring than it had once been, but Adam and Sarah seemed to like the game. Shadow decided that if his new humans had a backyard, he'd play fetch with them for as long as he could stand. He'd do anything, if it made them happy.

Shadow was so absorbed in imagining his new life that he almost didn't see Adam walk by again. Unable to help himself, he gave the man an excited bark. *Home!* Adam kept walking though, pretending not to hear. That when Shadow noticed the puppy in tow. An adorable little lab, with paws too big for his legs and a head too big for his neck. He gazed up at everything in wonder, occasionally tripping over his own paws. His collar, which was too big for him, was secured to a long leash. The other end of the leash rested firmly in Adam's grip.

Adam spoke to a disappointed-looking Kim, who had followed him back from the puppy kennels. Despite the dissonant barking that echoed down the hall, Shadow managed to catch a few of Adam's words. "… and so we decided we were really just set on a puppy. This little guy fits our lifestyle better…"

Shadow sat back on his haunches, staring down the hall in disbelief. So, that was it then. Two weeks of waffling on whether or not to take *him* home, but only ten minutes to pick out a puppy.

He turned and retreated to the back of the kennel, climbed into bed, and slumped down with his nose in the corner. *Why didn't anyone want him?* He was a good dog. Annie told him so almost every day. *So why wasn't he good enough to go home?*

It was Annie's day off, so Kim took it upon herself to comfort Shadow. She was by his side within minutes, stroking the fur on his back.

"I'm so sorry Shadow," she sighed. "I was hoping maybe you wouldn't notice what happened. I really thought he was here to take you home.

"I want you to know it was nothing to do with you. Nothing's your fault. There is nothing wrong with you, okay baby?"

Shadow tuned her out. Kim was a friend, but he didn't want to see any friends just then. He wasn't sure he even wanted to see Annie. He just wanted to be alone. Shadow retreated deep inside of himself, blocking out the rest of the world. It was a skill he'd learned well when Brian had abandoned him. Being alone made it much easier to wallow in sadness.

He wasn't sure when Kim left, but she eventually must have gotten tired of being ignored. No one bothered to try walking Shadow that day, which was fine with him. They knew he wasn't planning to leave the corner.

During the afternoon feeding, someone gave Shadow an extra scoop of food in hopes that it would cheer him up. He ate every last bit of it, but it didn't help, so he returned to his corner and waited for sleep. Sleep never came, of course, so Shadow passed the hours by staring at the wall. When someone came to tell him good night before closing the shelter, he pretended to be asleep just so he wouldn't have to look at them.

When darkness finally arrived, Shadow welcomed it. Night had a way of bringing a sense of isolation to the shelter, quieting the barking and sending the humans home. Except for the patch of moonlight streaming through the kennel's window, the darkness did a pretty good job of obscuring Shadow's vision, too. The isolation suited him perfectly. He stared at the wall in front of his face for what must have been hours, even after darkness prevented him from seeing it. *Why didn't anyone want him? He could be good, if they would only give him a chance.*

A familiar click at the end of the hall caused Shadow's ears to prick up, but he found himself hoping Annie hadn't come to comfort him. He really *did* just want to be by himself.

Shadow sat up, suddenly alarmed. Something wasn't right. It certainly sounded like Annie, but her footsteps came too fast. The rhythm was off, and she didn't make any attempts to shush the barking dogs. However, what *really* worried Shadow was the smell drifting down the hallway. The only other time a human had smelled that way was the day Brian had fallen while running. That scent meant pain, worry, and fear.

Shadow stood to greet Annie when she entered the kennel, all self-pity replaced with concern. Annie immediately collapsed on the floor, burying her face in Shadow's fur. Muffled sobs came from her mouth. Tears left mascara stains on Shadow's neck, but he remained perfectly still. He had been through enough crying episodes with Brian's children that he knew exactly what to do: hold back on the worried growls, and let the humans cry it out. Humans always felt better after crying. For all Shadow cared, Annie could pour every tear she had into his fur. He wouldn't tell anyone.

Annie's sobs grew heavier, and she wrapped her arms around Shadow's neck. Breathing through fur must have been too difficult to be practical, because she eventually lifted her head for fresh air. That was when Shadow identified another scent on her. Dry, and several minutes old, but unmistakable. *Blood.*

Just when Shadow thought Annie was done crying, another round of violent sobs wracked her body. She pushed her face deep into Shadow's side again, and he waited as patiently as possible. The scent of blood made patience much more difficult though. Something was very wrong. Shadow had always been gentle, but his fur bristled at the idea of someone hurting Annie. He wondered if they were still out there, lurking in the dark. Silently, he dared the attacker to follow Annie inside. They would find out exactly how much power still remained in an old dog's jaws.

Shadow waited for Annie's sobs to fade to a quiet series of whimpers before he pulled away. The moonlight cast an eerie glow across her face, but he could see it well enough. Annie's left eye was swollen shut, and a blotchy bruise had formed just below the eye. The scent of dried blood came from a gash in the middle of the bruise, perhaps made by a ring.

He smelled the man on her then, and Shadow knew all he needed to know. Fury boiled up inside of him. He turned to lunge at the door, find a way out, and find the man who hurt his friend. Annie's voice stopped him.

"I'm—" Her voice caught in her throat and she heaved, threatening to burst into tears all over again. Shadow's anger vanished, and he turned back to her. Patiently, he sat and held her gaze until she managed to find words again.

"I'm sorry," she said. "I know it's kind of silly, but I wanted to see you. You're such a good listener.

"I just don't understand what happened Shadow!" Annie's voice cracked. "Hunter's such a gentleman until he's drunk. Everything was so good before I ever saw him drunk.

"I don't even remember how the fight started. We were at his house. He was drinking, but I decided not to because I had to drive home. Then we were shouting, and we got in each other's faces, and all of the sudden he—"

Annie's voice broke off. Shadow inched closer, waiting for her to finish.

"He *hit* me!"

The tears started again. Annie's next words came slowly, broken up by sobs.

"Hard, Shadow! I didn't even have time to process it. He just swung a fist at me, without warning."

Annie's face twisted again and sobs won out over words. She closed her good eye and let the tears run down her face, unable to speak. Shadow just stared at her, unsure of what else to do. Seconds ticked by, each one marked by fresh tears. *He didn't want Annie to cry.*

Moving slowly so he didn't hurt her, Shadow leaned forward and licked at one of the tears on Annie's cheek. She cried even harder, but Shadow didn't stop. He licked at Annie's face as energetically as possible, even when the tears decreased in size and number. Strange sounds came from her mouth then—laughs, interspersed with sobs. Shadow didn't stop licking until every tear was gone and every sob was replaced by a laugh. Annie pulled away and wrapped her arms around Shadow's neck, staring at him through her open eye.

"You're so good." Annie managed a weak smile. "I'm sorry for freaking out on you buddy. It's just that the shelter was right on the way home, and before I even realized it, I was pulling into the parking lot."

Shadow stared at his friend, still concerned.

"Don't worry," she said. "I left right after he hit me, and he let me go."

Annie pulled a sleeve over her hand and dragged it across her eyes. "It's not even that it hurts that much anymore. It's just throbbing a little. But I was so scared, Shadow. He isn't a very big man, but he's bigger than me. After the first hit, I was so worried that the blows were going to keep coming. He just looked so angry, so out of control. For a minute, I thought he was going to kill me."

She shifted, pressing her back against the wall. Then she folded her arms across her chest and sighed. "I guess we both had a pretty rotten day today, huh buddy? Kim texted me and told me about Adam. I'm so sorry."

Shadow whined. He didn't want to think about Adam just then.

"Come here, buddy," said Annie. She patted the ground, and Shadow plodded over to her side. He sunk to the floor, resting his head on her leg. They stayed that way for a long time, with Annie slowly scratching Shadow's favorite spot. He was almost asleep when she spoke again.

"I just don't know what to do now. Do I break up with him? He really is a good guy when he isn't drunk. Maybe I should just stay with him and tell him he's not allowed to drink around me anymore."

Shadow lifted his head and growled.

Annie seemed startled for a moment, but then she understood. She always understood. "I know. I knew the moment I left his house tonight. I just didn't want to say it. I probably shouldn't ever see him again, should I? It's not like I have anything to pick up from his house, anyway."

Shadow didn't move. He just stared at Annie, waiting for her to understand again. She sighed, tears brimming in her open eye.

"Yeah. I know. You're right, buddy."

A single tear escaped Annie's eye and rolled down her cheek, but Shadow licked it away before it could drop to the ground.

Chapter 11

"Aww, look at that bunny!" said Annie, then quickly added, "Don't chase him."

Shadow panted at Annie, unfazed by the command. He hadn't been planning to chase the bunny anyway.

He and Annie were almost finished with their walk, and had only a minute or two left before they reached the shelter. Annie had seemed happier during the walk than she had been all day, although her mood was still somewhat subdued. The swelling in her eye had improved remarkably in the three days since the incident with Hunter. A scab and a blotchy purple stain still covered part of her face, but at least both eyes were open.

The warm weather and nearby forest sounds seemed to have helped both of their moods, because Shadow was feeling a little better too. He'd allowed himself some time to pout about Adam and Sarah over the last few days, since Annie hadn't been at work. As soon as she was back though, it was time to be done pouting. He needed to be strong for his friend.

Annie spent most of the walk pointing out little creatures in the branches or remarking about how warm the sun was. She seemed ready to talk about anything that wasn't Hunter, but she finally broached the subject near the end of the walk.

"I finally did it last night, Shadow. I made sure it was over the phone so he couldn't blow up at me again. I told myself I couldn't get up from the kitchen table until I finally called him, so I sat there for almost an hour working up the courage to do it. I told myself it was irrational to be scared, but I was so worried that he'd drive over to my apartment and start hitting me again.

"I finally told myself that the doors were locked, I had Cam and Ollie with me, and Hunter was probably sober anyway. So, I just called and told him that it was over and I never wanted to see him again. He was quiet for a long time, until I finally begged him to say something. And then he got so mad, Shadow. It scared me, even through the phone. He started yelling about how it was one little mistake and how I was overreacting. He even got to the point where he started suggesting that I made the whole thing up. I hung up before he finished, and I didn't answer when he tried to call again.

"I don't know if that was immature. Hitting me was immature too though. And trying to gaslight me about the whole thing…that's almost scarier than the fact that he hit me. I keep looking for some kind of sign I missed, some kind of indication that he was going to be like this. But I can't think of any. He *wasn't* like this until a few weeks ago, and I just don't get it. I just want to be done thinking about him, and I'm glad I cut him off. I was worried he was going to talk me into going back to him, you know? Even after what he did, it's going to be hard."

Shadow stared up at Annie, panting. He was proud of her, and he was glad she wasn't ever going to see that man again. Humans who hit each other were the same as humans who hit dogs: it was never just a one-time thing.

As usual, Annie seemed perfectly in tune with Shadow's thoughts. "Oh, and I think it's probably a bad idea to try and have him adopt you now. And I'm not just saying that because I'm mad at him. It's just that if he was willing to hurt me, he'd probably be willing to hurt you, too. Violence isn't limited to just one species. It's all kind of the same, you know?"

That had been a given, as far as Shadow was concerned. Being hit by an out of control human was *not* the future he wanted, and he didn't want to be with someone who had hurt his friend, anyway.

Annie held the shelter's back door open and then led Shadow through each of the following sets of doors. She returned him to his kennel and offhandedly mentioned that he might get some time in the dog run that afternoon, if it sounded good. It sounded *very* good to Shadow, so he licked Annie's hand while she removed his leash.

She had almost closed the gate on Shadow's kennel when the door at the end of the hall slammed open. Dogs all over the hallway immediately started to bark, and Shadow and Annie both whirled to see what was happening. A man strode down the hall, making a beeline for Annie. His fists were clenched, as was his jaw. Bloodshot eyes were set deep into his face under a head of short blonde hair. Shadow had never seen the man before, but recognized the scent instantly. *Hunter.*

Shadow shot a glance at Annie, who seemed to have frozen in place with her hand still against the partially-open kennel door. Just then, she seemed to find herself and dropped her hand to her side. She appeared relaxed, but Shadow could still hear her heart's frantic rhythm from several feet away.

"Hunter…" she said cautiously.

Hunter stopped only a few steps away, his breath reeking of liquor. "It was an accident, Annie! You've got to trust me!"

Annie's fist clenched at her side. Hunter took another step. When he spoke again, every desperate syllable slurred into the next.

"Please, Annie. You can't throw away all we have based on one little night. You don't want to look back in twenty years and realize you lost me over an exaggeration. It won't happen again!"

Annie opened her mouth, but Hunter pressed on. "Don't you remember our first date? We went to that little Thai place with the name neither of us could pronounce. We were both so nervous, and you could barely speak until I admitted *I* was nervous, and then it was like everything was perfect between us, and then…we became best friends that night, Annie.

"We've had so many experiences that are so much more important than what happened Saturday. Why aren't you focusing on those as much as you're focusing on Saturday? Think about all the walks with Cam and Ollie, or the movies we watched at my place, and how you almost always fell asleep on my shoulder before the movie was done, and that day in the rain—"

Annie interrupted him. "Hunter…"

"I love you, Annie!"

Annie stepped back, apparently startled. The voices of barking dogs rushed in to fill the silence, and Annie had to speak over them when she found her words again. She stood firm, but Shadow detected a hint of a quiver in her speech.

"No, Hunter. You don't punch people you love."

Hunter looked startled, just as Annie had a moment earlier. Then his face twisted into a snarl. The barking rose to a cacophony. Deb and Anthony burst through the door, sprinting down the hall. Only Shadow remained perfectly silent, watching Hunter's every move.

"I made *one* mistake!" Hunter screamed. "That fight was your fault anyway, and you completely blew everything out of proportion. You wouldn't exaggerate so much if you knew what it was like to *really* get hit, Annie! You want to know what it's like? You wanna see how ridiculous you're being? DO YOU WANT TO KNOW?"

He raised a hand to strike. Annie flinched only a little, staring stoically ahead instead of turning away. Deb and Anthony increased their pace, but anyone could see that they would never make it in time.

With a noise that can only be described as a roar, Shadow barged through his kennel's gate. He leapt between Hunter and Annie, ignoring the jarring pain that shot through his knees when he landed.

The humans froze. The barking dogs fell silent. Only Shadow moved, snarling up at Hunter. Hunter didn't lash out right away, but his eyes burned with barely contained fury. Shadow knew the man's fist could come crashing down at any moment, but he wasn't afraid. Only angry. *Leave her alone!*

Hunter refused to back away from Annie, which only served to further enrage Shadow. He raised every inch of fur on his back, until he looked more like a small wolf than a dog. A growl rose from deep in his throat, revealing every gleaming inch of his teeth as it left his mouth. The teeth weren't as sharp as they once were, but they were still sharp enough. Shadow snapped them together, punctuating every growl with the clash of teeth in case Hunter had any misconceptions about what they could do.

That seemed to do it. The change Shadow had been looking for appeared in Hunter's eyes: that subtle shift in the pupils, a slight quiver of the eyebrows. His anger was gone, swallowed up by fear. Slowly, he took exactly one step back.

Shadow took exactly one step forward.

Shadow paused when he heard sirens outside. It took several more seconds for Hunter to recognize the noise, but his eyes grew wide when he finally did. He whirled around, retreating down the hall so fast he was almost running. Shadow didn't give chase, but he made sure to let out a menacing growl every time the man glanced over his shoulder.

Hunter disappeared through the door, but Shadow's ears told him everything eyesight couldn't. A new voice that could only belong to the police officer. Slurred protests. Deb's voice, angry and rushed. Clinking handcuffs. Shadow's teeth remained bared until Hunter's drunken voice moved outside and the door slammed shut behind him.

Shadow tensed when a hand touched his back, but it was only Annie. She smoothed out his fur, knelt in front of him. Annie reeked of fear, so Shadow wagged his tail to let her know everything was okay. He hoped he hadn't scared her.

As the color returned to Annie's face, she pressed her forehead against Shadow's. A hand stroked the side of his neck, shaking only a little.

Annie let out the breath she'd been holding. "That was really scary, buddy. You didn't have to do that though. I don't want you getting hurt, okay? You don't need to put yourself in harm's way for me."

After a long pause, she added, "Thank you." Then she wrapped her arms around his neck and didn't let go.

Chapter 12

The snowman was perfect. Or, as perfect as a snowman made in only two inches of snow could be. Bel and Bri had used nearly all of the snow in the yard to make it, and despite the fact that it contained almost as much grass as snow, they were proud of their creation.

The children posed on either side of their snowman while Brian pulled up the camera on his phone. Shadow was there too, seated just in front of Brian and trying his very best to restrain himself.

He failed.

Just as the camera clicked, Shadow rushed in and lunged for the snowman's nose. He ripped the carrot free, and the snowman's face exploded into a million tiny snowflakes. Cries of dismay came from the children, who immediately began to pursue Shadow. Eating while fleeing was a skill any smart dog learned early in life though, so the carrot never stood a chance.

Once Shadow had finished eating, he sat and gave the children his open-mouthed smile. He *loved* carrots. They were the only vegetable he liked, in fact.

Bel had some especially harsh words for Shadow, but Brian defended him, explaining that dogs didn't know any better. Then with a gentle laugh, he put Shadow inside so the children could reconstruct their snowman's head. When it was done, they used a rock for the nose instead of a carrot.

Shadow woke up and blinked the sun out of his eyes. The light streaming through the kennel's window had moved from his belly to his face, making it much too bright to sleep.

Yawning, Shadow rolled over and shook himself off before limping to his food bowl. The dream had amused him, despite the pain of remembering his old family. He remembered that day well. Four winters ago, on the year's first day of snow. He'd been younger, and didn't possess quite the same sense of control he'd learned since then. His younger self's antics had been *quite* entertaining.

Dreams were the only places Shadow still ran. The long months since the incident with Hunter had been quiet and uneventful, but the time spent in the kennel had still taken its toll on his knees. Despite daily walks and the time out in the dog run, Shadow's arthritis had progressed at such an alarming rate that Anthony had recently put him on a small dose of pain medication. When the shelter volunteers first started hiding the pills in his food, Shadow had diligently eaten around them. However, that only led to the pills being stuffed down his throat later, so he quickly decided it would just be easier to eat what was in the dish. The medicine helped some, but not much.

Seeing that his food bowl was empty, Shadow sat down by the gate. It was nearly time to go out to the dog run, and he couldn't wait to bask in the sun by Riley's side. He and Riley had been allowed outside nearly every day during the summer, since the warm sun seemed to ease the stiffness in their joints. As far as Shadow was concerned though, it was Riley that made the trips outside truly worthwhile. Her gentle presence was more comforting than the sun could ever hope to be.

When Annie finally came to take Shadow outside, he panted with excitement. Annie had seemed happier over the past few months, and there hadn't been any more incidents with Hunter. She had tried to explain that Hunter couldn't see her anymore because of something called a restraining order, but Shadow couldn't quite understand all of the details. Not that it mattered, as long as Annie was safe. Her black eye was fully healed, the gash had faded into a pale scar, and they had taken plenty of wonderful walks together during the course of the summer.

Annie held the door open and Shadow stepped out into the dog run. He headed for the spot where he always met with Riley, but then stopped in his tracks. Riley wasn't there, but that didn't make any sense. Riley *always* went out to the dog run before Shadow did. Every time he arrived, she was already waiting in their sunny spot.

Shadow limped around the edges of the dog run, but couldn't find Riley anywhere. Traces of her scent lingered in the napping spot, but they were at least a day old. Confused, Shadow settled down to wait for his friend.

Annie sighed and crossed the dog run. She sat on the ground next to Shadow, resting a hand on his back before sighing again. She had her bad news smell on, which made him nervous. *Something was wrong.*

"Hey buddy, I have something to tell you. Riley...she's not here anymore. She was really old, and she got sick last night...do you understand?

"I'm sorry buddy. I know you really loved her."

Shadow didn't fully understand, but he got the message. Riley was gone.

He rested his chin on the ground and shut his eyes. That old, familiar heartache had already started seeping into his chest. It wasn't overpowering, the way it had been when Brian abandoned him, but it would grow. The longer Shadow went without Riley, the more he would miss her.

Annie scratched the back of Shadow's neck. "I have to go in and get some work done, buddy. But I'll be back out when I can. I promise."

Shadow sighed in acknowledgement, but didn't move when Annie got up to leave. Suddenly, being outside didn't sound fun anymore. Several dogs played on the other side of the run, but their youthful energy didn't bring Shadow any of the joy it should have. Riley was gone. So was her comforting presence, her steady breathing at his side. Every scent felt suddenly fainter, every sound a little farther off. Losing Riley was about more than just losing a friend. It was losing part of what made life loveable.

After a time, Shadow slipped off to sleep and spent the afternoon drifting in and out of consciousness. The warm summer sun made napping easy, but it felt all wrong without Riley at his side. That was where she belonged, and her absence left Shadow cold and exposed.

Annie returned after an indeterminable amount of time, waking Shadow up from a horrible dream where Riley was somewhere off in the woods, barking for help. Annie's hands stroked Shadow's neck, and she gently cradled his head in her lap. She didn't say anything, but her presence was enough. She understood that.

After drifting off to sleep a few more times, Shadow looked up and gave Annie a few halfhearted licks. The sun's position told him it must be close to closing time at the shelter, but Annie made no move to get up.

She gave Shadow a grim smile. "I know this isn't the best time, buddy, but I have something else to tell you. I'm not going to be able to take you home. I'm really sorry. I think I kinda convinced myself it would happen.

"I talked to my landlord twice, but she didn't budge. I threatened to move, but I'm not really in any position to break a lease and she knows it. I offered to pay extra rent, but she still said no. 'Two dogs per apartment, *max*,' she said. Then she gave me this lecture about making exceptions to the rules and how if she does something for me, she has to do it for everyone. Sounded like my mom back when I was in high school.

"There might be some houses that let people have more than two dogs, but I really can't afford a house. I'm really sorry buddy. I just can't make it work. I wish I could."

Shadow didn't understand much about landlords or leasing agreements, but Annie's voice told him she really was sorry. He hadn't ever really expected to go home with Annie, because she'd made it clear a long time ago that she couldn't do it. The important thing was that Annie *couldn't* take him home, rather than *wouldn't*. Shadow understood that much, and he still loved her all the same.

Annie straightened, jostling Shadow's head around in her lap. "You're going to get adopted though, buddy. This morning I went to Deb and sponsored your adoption fee. That means whoever adopts you now doesn't have to pay a cent. I'll be paying it instead. Shots, a leash, and you, all for free. No one can resist that, right?"

She smiled at Shadow, and this time the smile was real. Annie's optimism was contagious, and no setback could keep her down for very long. Gazing up at her face, Shadow couldn't help but feel a trickle of warmth. If there was anyone who could lessen the pain of losing Riley, it was Annie.

"Next week is the Fall Adoption Fair. We do it every September. It's three days long and it's our biggest adoption event of the year. I didn't work here back then, but I hear that four years ago, every single dog in the shelter got adopted. If you don't get adopted by the time the fair comes around, I *know* someone will take you home then. Just hang in there, buddy."

Chapter 13

The Fall Adoption Fair was an even bigger event than Annie had described. The entire thing took place at City Park, so the dogs were to be transported by a fleet of volunteer vehicles. Annie made Shadow promise to be good every day for the week leading up to it.

On the morning of the first day, an army of humans showed up to ferry dogs to and from the park. Before the sun was even up, dogs were being led out of the long hallway in what may have been the most chaotic spectacle Shadow had ever seen. Most dogs caused trouble, pulling on their leashes or barking loudly. Shadow tried to set a good example for the younger dogs, since Annie had asked him to do so. It didn't seem to do much good, but he still sat patiently at the front of his kennel and padded softly after Annie when his turn came.

Out in the parking lot, Annie opened the door to a beat-up SUV and lifted Shadow inside. The inability to get in and out of cars without help was embarrassing, but Shadow didn't mind as long as it was Annie doing the lifting. As he positioned himself in a seat, a twinge of puppy excitement leaped into Shadow's heart. He hadn't been in a car for a very long time, and car rides often lead to wonderful adventures. Even better, *this* car smelled like Annie.

Shadow sniffed at one of the seats to make certain the car belonged to Annie, and she gave him a quick pat on the back. "That's right buddy. I made sure you were with me."

Annie closed the door and went back into the shelter, so Shadow occupied himself by sniffing around the interior of the car. The scent of old shoes emanated from the trunk, mingling with the dusty scent of the seats. Annie's dogs' scents were there too. Ollie's excitement and Cam's patience lingered on every surface of the car, and lost strands of their fur had become embedded in the seats. No doubt Annie took them for all sorts of adventures in the car.

By the time Annie returned and swung into the driver's seat, Shadow shared the back with two other dogs. Annie introduced them to each other while she started the car. The pit bull to Shadow's left was named Mango, while the beagle on his right was named Scott. Annie seemed to find it amusing that Scott was a girl, but Shadow didn't mind. He had never understood why humans thought boys and girls weren't allowed to have the same kinds of names anyway.

Annie's voice dropped off when they reached the exit to the parking lot. She waited for an oncoming truck to pass, then touched the accelerator with her foot. The car's tires briefly slipped on a patch of loose gravel, but then the vehicle lurched onto the road and picked up speed. Annie squinted into the rising sun for a few moments, but finally gave in and reached for a pair of sunglasses.

"I ended up with three of you because you're all so well behaved," she said. "Most other cars could only take one dog, maybe two.

"You should all be proud! You're the best-behaved dogs in the shelter! So stay on your best behavior at the park too, okay?"

The ride to the park was short, but Shadow made the most of it by taking in every tree and house that whizzed by. He had always loved car rides. When he had been younger, Brian would roll down the windows so Shadow could lean out. With the wind whipping past his fur, he felt like he could fly.

Annie snapped Shadow out of his daydream by suddenly cranking up the radio and shouting "I *love* this *song*!" She danced in her seat, shoulders bobbing up and down. Without moving her gaze from the road, she shouted, "Sing, puppies!" and launched into an exaggerated version of the song from the radio. Mango offered a couple of encouraging barks when Annie missed a high note, but other than that, none of the puppies sang. As soon as the park came into view, Annie stopped singing and dancing, apparently too embarrassed to let any other humans see the performance. With a straight face and firm gaze, she whipped the car into a parking space. Then she glanced in the rearview mirror and said, "Alright puppies! I want an empty car when I go home today! I want you all to get adopted!"

She collected the dogs from the back and walked all three of them to the center of the park. The amount of planning that had obviously gone into the event was breathtaking. The whole thing had been set up facing a long stretch of sidewalk, so that both intentional adopters and passersby would see the dogs. Countless portable dog pens, most of them already occupied, had been linked together in the grass. Five evenly spaced pop-up tents stood at regular intervals in front of the pens, serving as either bases for volunteers or shelter for the dogs if the weather turned bad.

Annie directed Shadow, Scott, and Mango into three adjacent pens and then took her place under a nearby tent. Shadow's pen contained everything a dog could possibly need for a day outside—food, water, even a new toy. He happily rolled in the grass that made up the floor of his pen, covering himself in the scent. Just the feeling of fresh grass beneath his paws was enough to make this a good day.

Two more dogs passed by Shadow's pen, and he stood to watch them. It seemed like nearly every dog at the shelter had come to the park. There was no way to count them all, but it must have been more dogs than Shadow had ever seen in one place before. And after the dogs were all in place, humans began to arrive. Annie had been right about the size of the event. *There were even more people than there were dogs!* Countless people—most seeming friendly enough—stopped by Shadow's kennel for a visit. Shadow was on his feet the entire day, meeting new people, sniffing new hands, and playing with as much energy as he could muster. Fortunately, the pen was small enough that he had an excuse not to run.

Annie was busy all day too, pacing between pens and answering questions. She talked to potential adopters for most of the day, but Shadow was so busy that he only caught little glimpses of what she said. "Yes, we have an 88% placement rate for animals that come into our shelter—the highest in the state... This is Shadow. He's such a gentleman... yes, Scott is a girl...Okay well, after you think about it, you can always come back tomorrow or give us a call at this number... Yes sir, we always encourage adoption over breeding, because breeding operations just don't have the animals' best interests at heart. Plus, there are plenty of animals who need homes already..."

The flurry of visiting humans were relentless with their questions for Annie, which kept her away from Shadow for most of the day. Occasionally she was able to give him a few quick scratches while introducing him to some humans, but then she was gone again, off to process some adoption form or answer a question.

By late afternoon, Shadow was too tired to keep standing. He settled down into the grass, nearly taking a headfirst tumble when he tried to bend his aching knees. People still came and he still greeted them just as happily, so Shadow decided it would be alright to stay down for the rest of the day. The afternoon sun warmed his back, and he splayed out to soak up as many rays as he could. The sun's rays inevitably brought on thoughts of Riley, which brought hints of that old ache back to Shadow's chest. It was impossible not to think of her whenever the sun came out. There were plenty of other dogs to befriend, but none of them seemed content to simply nap with Shadow all day, and none of them could replace Riley. The sun wasn't quite as warm without her.

Shadow was exhausted by the time Annie lifted him back into her car at the end of the day. Mango joined him in the car seat, but Scott was gone. Shadow vaguely remembered seeing a human take the little beagle home at some point during the day, but it was difficult to remember when.

Annie climbed into the front seat and turned around to face Shadow and Mango. She looked worn out from the day too. Her face was sunburned, despite the copious amounts of sunscreen she'd put on in the morning. There was a hint of disappointment in her eyes, although she wore a smile. Shadow and Mango must have looked disappointed too, because Annie patted them and said, "Hey, cheer up guys! I know it was tiring, but the first day's always the busiest!"

She quickly added, "But don't worry, you both still have a great chance of going home! There won't be as many people tomorrow, but a *lot* of dogs went home today. Do the math, and that means you'll both get more attention!"

Shadow couldn't imagine having even *more* attention than he'd already received, but he vowed to do whatever it took to find a home.

****

Annie was right. The second day of the fair wasn't as busy, but Shadow somehow *did* get more attention. He wondered how Annie always managed to be right about everything. She seemed to have a knack for that.

Each person stayed with Shadow for longer, even climbing into his pen to sit in the grass with him. Shadow liked everyone he met, but for different reasons. There was a young man who looked like Adam, which made Shadow both excited and nervous. He smelled different from Adam, so Shadow decided it was alright to like him. A human with glasses had a gentle, soothing voice. A couple of young boys, while slightly irritating, seemed to have unlimited quantities of love to give.

The younger boy even reminded Shadow of little Bri, who had always left him with kisses.

One man who sat in the pen was a rare type of human—he allowed Shadow to give his face as many licks as he pleased. He sat in the pen with Shadow so long that the top of his bald head went from white to red, but eventually he got up and left. *Everyone* eventually got up and left, no matter how much affection Shadow showed them. Both Annie and Kim had told him in the past that there was nothing wrong with him, but Shadow couldn't help but wonder if that was really true.

In the afternoon, one young girl read to Shadow while her mother spoke with Annie. She was at the age where she read anything in sight, so Shadow heard everything written on his pen's namecard at least twice. The girl stumbled over the occasional word, but Shadow waited patiently while she sounded it out. He'd been through this before plenty of times, back when Bel had learned to read. Shadow had been told repeatedly that he was the best listener in the family, a title he took pride in.

"Shadow," said the girl. "Male shep-herd mix. Sixty-eight pounds. Twelve…years old. Wow, that's older than Michael! Michael is my brother. You don't know him."

She glanced back at the card, using her finger to keep track of the lines. "Shadow is an older…gentle…man who would love to go home with you. His add… his adopt…"

The girl furrowed her brow, confused. Shadow poked his nose out of the pen and gave her hand an encouraging lick.

"His adop-tie-on fee has already been paid by a...gen-er-ous sponsor. Ask a... staff member for dee-ta-ils."

The girl stepped back, looking rather pleased with herself. Just then, her mother turned away from Annie and said, "Ready to go, Jenna?"

Jenna stared up at her mother. "Are we taking Shadow home?"

Jenna's mother gave her a weak smile. "Maybe. We need to look at other dogs too. Shadow might be a little big for our house."

The young girl nodded and took her mother's hand. As they left, she pointed to a sign that hung from a pop-up tent and read, "Save a life. Adopt a... home-less dog."

They worked their way farther down the line of pens, stopping to visit several dogs along the way. Eventually, they went home with a dog that must have been a fifth of Shadow's size. Shadow sighed, settled down into the grass, and rested his head on his paws. It was hard not to get discouraged after watching so many other dogs go home.

Tired of meeting people and then watching them leave, Shadow distracted himself with a dancing blade of grass sprouting just in front of his nose. Any time he inhaled, the blade of grass leaned in and tickled his face. It leaned away again when Shadow exhaled, which he found quite amusing.

When Annie directed a couple toward Shadow's pen, he left his blade of grass and made sure to play with the humans. He played with every human he met, which was quite the achievement considering how many of them there were. At the end of the day though, Shadow found himself back in Annie's car. When Mango didn't join them, Annie explained that the pit bull had been adopted at the last minute before closing. Shadow sighed. *Other dogs always seemed to be able to find homes.*

The third day was like the first two days, but only in the morning. Dark clouds rolled in around midday, and before long a cold, heavy rain began to fall from the sky. The tent closest to Shadow's pen was moved to shelter him, so he managed to stay mostly dry. The rain scared off most of the potential adopters though, which discouraged Shadow even more. The only advantage of the rainstorm was that Annie's table of adoption paperwork also had to stay under the tent, which in turn meant that Annie was close by for most of the day. She stood next to Shadow's pen, scratching the top of his head and waiting for more people to come by. While they waited, Annie told Shadow more stories.

This rainstorm was supposed to last all the way through until tomorrow morning, she told him. At least it wasn't snow, but it sure came at a bad time.

Annie told Shadow about a rainstorm from when she was a very little girl. The rainstorm lasted for three days and nights, and the streets got so flooded that school was canceled on the third day. Annie laughed. "We didn't get any snow days that entire year, I remember. But we did get a rain day. That's the only one I've ever had."

When it was finally time to pack things up, Annie led Shadow through the rain and back to the car. The water soaked them both long before they reached the car, and Shadow decided that the weather reflected his mood pretty well. *How was he supposed to find a happy home if no one even gave him a chance?*

Shadow hoisted his front half into the car while Annie helped with the back half. Always prepared, she grabbed a towel from the trunk and stood in the rain while she dried him off. Rain fell onto the seat while Annie stood in the open doorway, but she didn't seem to notice. She looked as disappointed as Shadow felt.

Sighing, Annie stepped away and reached back to close the door. Shadow whined.

Annie paused, and then leaned into the car again. Outside, the rain soaked through what little bit of dry clothing she still had, but she didn't seem to care. Instead, she scratched both sides of Shadow's neck in big, slow circles. Then she pressed her forehead against his and let out another sigh.

"I'm really sorry, buddy. I was so sure you were going to go home this weekend. The rain was some really bad luck. We're going to keep trying though. You don't deserve to have to stay in that kennel."

She waited there with Shadow for a long time, her head pressed against his, neither of them moving. Rain streamed in through the open car door and soaked the seat, but they were both too miserable to notice.

Finally, Annie stood back and looked at Shadow. Her voice took on an optimistic tone, but her eyes betrayed her.

"Listen, buddy. The foster system has been full all year so far, but we adopted all but eight dogs this weekend. There's going to be a lot of rearranging of dogs and a lot of them will be coming out of foster and back into the shelter to get adopted. I think there's a good chance of getting you into a foster home. It isn't a permanent home, but it is a home. And it'll buy you some more time, so you don't get…it'll be good for you."

Annie shut the door and climbed into the front seat. Neither one of them made a sound during the ride back to the shelter.

Chapter 14

Shadow never made it to a foster home.

The rain that started on the last day of the adoption fair turned out to be an even bigger storm than the one from Annie's story. Heavy rain drummed against the shelter's roof for five days and four nights.

During the storm—and in the weeks after—the shelter was the busiest Shadow had ever seen it. Countless dogs and cats were displaced in the floods, pushing every shelter in the area past capacity. On the fourth day of rain, Shadow heard talk of another shelter being practically destroyed in a flash flood. Fortunately, they had managed to save every animal in a miracle involving an army of community members. Shadow had been glad to hear that, even though every single dog from the destroyed shelter ended up in his shelter.

Shadow missed his walks several days in a row, which made him hate the rain. Annie explained that they couldn't go out because the creek near the trail had flooded, but knowing the reason didn't ease Shadow's restlessness. After the second day without a walk, he started occupying himself by pacing the kennel and watching the endless parade of new dogs go by. They were brought in every hour of the day, straight from the grooming room. "Flood dogs," they were called. Some were reclaimed by their worried guardians within a few days, but fresh waves of homeless dogs quickly took their places.

Staff worked longer hours to handle the volume, volunteers showed up for longer days, and the nearly empty shelter quickly swelled to capacity again. Since the shelter filled up so quickly, the foster dogs stayed in their foster homes. And Shadow stayed in the shelter.

The days grew shorter as they passed, each a little colder than the last one. Shadow's naps in the warm sun grew shorter too, since the sun spent so much less time in the sky. Some days, when the staff determined that it was too cold to go out for more than a few minutes, there were no naps in the sun at all.

As the weeks ticked by, even Shadow's beloved walks decreased in length. Not because of the weather—Annie and Kim were always prepared for bad weather—but simply because Shadow's legs didn't work quite the way they once had. His joints ached and his muscles tired quickly, despite the fact that he did little to tire them out. Once, Anthony had observed that daily walks were probably the best way to prevent the arthritis's progression. But by shortening Shadow's walks, the arthritis had somehow managed to prevent its own prevention.

Annie did the best she could to ease Shadow's aging. She always made sure he received his medication and that his bed had extra blankets to pad his aching bones. She scratched his favorite spot and told him stories, or sat next to him on the floor of the common room when it was too cold for the dog run. One day in late autumn, the shelter was closed except for the basic staff needed to feed and care for the dogs. Annie made sure to visit though, appearing during the afternoon with someone she introduced as her sister. With a furtive glance to make sure no one was watching, Annie reached into her coat pocket, produced a small dinner roll, and whispered, "Happy Thanksgiving, buddy."

The dinner roll was delicious, and Shadow adored Annie's sister almost as much as he adored Annie. They had the same way of talking to him like he was a human, the same smile, and even the same laugh. Annie's sister repeatedly exclaimed that she wished Shadow could go with her, but they would never allow it in the dorms.

Shortly after that day, the cold grip of winter set in and all of Shadow's dog run time became common room time. Staff set up an artificial Christmas tree in a corner of the common room, which pleased Shadow even if it wasn't a real tree. It didn't bring the smell of the forest inside like the trees from Brian's house had, but it *was* nice for taking naps under.

On one particularly snowy morning, Shadow slept under the tree with more excitement than he thought possible. Outside, the first snow deep enough to dig in had fallen, and he couldn't *wait* for his afternoon walk. It had been far too long since he last played in snow. It was lucky that the cold had little effect on Shadow's joints, though he would have been excited regardless of that. *It would take more than arthritis to keep him away from his favorite weather.*

In between periods of sleep, Shadow listened to Annie make phone calls in the adoption office next to the common room. She usually played with the dogs on her days to supervise the common room, but she'd been on the phone all morning. Shadow could hear what she said clearly enough through the window between the two rooms, but he could only hear her side of the conversation.

"No, he hasn't shown any behavioral issues," said Annie. She paused while the other person spoke. "I understand, we're still full from the floods too. Just checking. Thank you for your time."

She hung up and quickly dialed another number. "Hi, my name is Annie Collins and I'm with the Ridgeview Dog Rescue. I'm calling to see if your shelter has any room for a dog who's almost out of time here. I'm told you've accepted dogs from us in the past.

"I know, I never thought the floods would still be affecting us after so long either. It's been a hard few months. Well, good luck and please call us if anything changes for you."

Shadow dozed off briefly while Annie searched for a new number to dial. He woke up halfway through another call, unsure of how much time had passed. Annie's voice seemed strained, as if being polite and cheerful was quickly becoming a chore.

"...No sir, our foster systems are completely full. Every time we adopt a dog out, another comes in almost immediately.

"That's a good idea, Utah escaped most of the flooding. I'll try calling around there. Thank you. You too."

Shadow fell asleep again while Annie began making calls to shelters in neighboring states. He slept lightly, waking every few moments to catch snippets of conversation.

"...they're *all* from a hoarding situation? Yes, I can understand why you have your hands full. Thank you. Please call me if anything changes."

"Hi, is this Harper's Hope Dog Rescue? Yes, I can hold."

"...only has a couple of weeks left here..."

"...Please call me if anything changes. Thank you."

Shadow wondered how many numbers Annie had dialed. Over time, her normally cheerful tone transformed into rushed, clipped speech and the calls grew more and more desperate. "Hi, this is a longshot but I'm with Ridgeview Dog Rescue and I'm looking to place a dog who's almost out of time, and I know your shelter usually takes dogs under twenty pounds, but if you have any space... Yes, of course. Thanks anyway."

"...been here a little over eleven months. What, unadoptable? No, he's really sweet. He just had some bad luck. Oh, *your* policy says he is. Well, thank you anyway. Bye."

Shadow rolled over and rested his silver muzzle on his paws. He tried to stay awake and listen to Annie, but his eyelids were just so heavy...

While he slept, Shadow dreamt that Riley was there in the common room with him. She slept soundly on the other side of the Christmas tree, but awakened when he licked her. Riley let out a greeting bark, her voice more full of life and energy than ever before. After their customary sniffing and greeting, the dogs spotted a bag of treats perched high in the tree. The treats were so close that Shadow could almost taste them, but they were just out of reach. He whined, but Riley didn't seem worried. She stretched high up and leaned against the tree, almost as if it were a human she hadn't seen in a while. *How could Riley stretch up like that?* Shadow wondered. *He couldn't even do that, and her arthritis was much worse than his.* By the time Shadow realized what his friend intended, the tree was already falling...

Shadow woke to the sound of Annie's muffled sobs. Worried, he skipped his customary post-nap shake and hurried to the office window, nearly knocking the tree over in the process. Annie sat at the desk in the office, head buried in her hands. Strands of hair curled in front of her face, strangled by clenching fingers. She shuddered with every breath, and worry raced into Shadow's heart. *What was wrong? Who hurt his friend?*

Humans didn't seem to like barking, but their hearing was just so *bad* that sometimes it was the only way to get their attention. So, Shadow barked. When Annie didn't react, he barked again.

Annie slowly lifted her head, turning to face the glass. She rose, pushed back her long strands of hair, and opened the door to the common room. She knelt in front of Shadow, hugging a knee close to her chest. The crying had stopped, but she still smelled like tears, and her eyes looked ready to overflow again at any given moment.

"Hey buddy," she finally managed.

Shadow started to sit, remembered that sitting hurt his knees, and stood back up. Then he focused on Annie again, giving her a concerned look.

"Sorry, I was just trying to find other shelters to take you in case..." she trailed off. During the silence, a dog with floppy ears walked over to sniff at Annie's shoe. He must not have found what he was looking for, because he turned and walked away again after only a few seconds.

"I don't want to scare you," Annie said. "But none of them had room. And our foster system is still full from the floods."

Annie's voice cracked. "It just isn't fair, buddy. You're such a good dog. I knew this happened, but I told myself it didn't happen so much at this shelter. There was a dog whose year ended when I first started here, but I barely knew her. And Riley... she was so good too, but she got sick. I've never seen healthy dogs like you have to..." She paused again to wipe away a tear that had spilled over the edge of her eye.

Shadow remembered the last time he'd seen Annie cry, just after Hunter had hit her. *What could possibly be that bad again?* That old unscratchable itch of worry cropped up in Shadow's chest. He whined at Annie, prompting her to rest a hand on his side.

"You know," she sniffed, "when I was a little girl, I said I was going to save all of the animals. All over the world. Some kids wanted to be an astronaut, or a doctor... I just wanted to help you all. All the dogs, and the cows, and the dolphins. I thought it would be easy to save every animal, because I thought grownups knew everything."

Another tear streamed down Annie's face, briefly hesitating above the scar left by Hunter before continuing down her cheek. She didn't bother to wipe it away, holding her palms out in frustration instead.

"And yet, now I'm all grown up and I just feel so… powerless. I mean, I rescued Cam and Ollie and I like to *think* I did some good by taking a job here but why is it so hard? I don't *know* what to do, Shadow. There has to be *something* I can do but I don't know what!"

Her hands returned to her face, and she let out a choking sob. Shadow forgot all of the other dogs in the room, forgot the rest of the shelter. Annie was his best friend in the world, and he couldn't stand to see her cry. He lifted a paw to Annie's face and used it to pull one of her hands away, careful not to scratch her. She covered her eyes again almost immediately, but after a second try, she let her hands fall to her sides. Then she stared at Shadow with the saddest look he'd ever seen. Tears covered her face, rolling down her cheeks in rivulets. Her bottom lip quivered, ready to curl downward and release a fresh wave of sobs at any moment.

Shadow couldn't stand it. He licked the salty tears away from her face, just as he had done the last time she cried. And, just like the last time, every lick slowly made Annie's sobs transform into laughter. Even the laugher was different this time though, strangled and laced with pain.

Annie stopped crying just long enough to throw her arms around Shadow's neck and hug him tight. He resisted the urge to squirm away from the hug, resting his chin on Annie's shoulder for a long time. When Annie finally spoke again, it was in a whisper, as if anything louder might cause her to burst into tears.

"What are we going to do, buddy?"

Chapter 15

Shadow gnawed on his new tennis ball, testing its springiness with rhythmic bites. *Bite down, spring back.* His old tennis ball had lost some of its springiness, but the new one was perfect. It had all of the bounce a ball should have, although he didn't particularly appreciate the way it left little green fluffs all over his tongue. *Bite down, spring back.*

He had received the ball two days ago, as a Christmas present. *Bite down, spring back.* The staff had left stockings outside of each dog's kennel, full of gifts Shadow could smell but couldn't see. On Christmas morning, they unloaded the contents of each stocking for the dogs, which caused more barking than Shadow had heard in his entire year at the shelter. In addition to the ball, Shadow received a candy-cane shaped dog treat that cracked between his jaws in an absolutely delightful way. *Bite down, spring back.*

It had been a good day—one of the best days at the shelter—and had provided some distraction from the normal monotony of the kennel. Still, Christmas at the shelter was painfully different from Christmas at home. Christmas day at Brian's house had always started early. Shadow helped the children tear open their presents, then helped them play with their new toys. The aromas of various foods drifted out of the kitchen, savory and sweet and greasy. Guests were usually over for dinner in the evening, which Shadow had always loved because guests were the most likely to sneak scraps to him at the table.

Last Christmas, the children had gotten a new puppy. And only a few days later, Brian left Shadow at the shelter. Shadow wondered if the new puppy was still at home. He even felt a twinge of worry for the noisy little dog. *They would love him well, but only until he got old and slow. Then who would love him?*

Shadow didn't like thinking about his old family, so perhaps it was a blessing that Christmas was so different at the shelter. After presents had been distributed and the morning cleaning and feeding was done, all of the humans went home to their families. There were no children to play with or table scraps to beg for at the shelter, although Annie snuck Shadow a roll on the following day.

Two days after Christmas, everything at the shelter was already back to normal. Normal cleaning, normal walks, normal food. The staff went home shortly after dark, so Shadow settled into his bed and waited for sleep to come. He tried to fall asleep with the springy new ball in his mouth, but that turned out to make breathing difficult. Instead, he settled for nesting the ball in a heap of blankets, folding his paws over it, and resting his chin on top of the whole pile. Someone at the shelter had decided that such an old dog might need more blankets to stay warm, but Shadow just used them for extra padding. He would rather be too cold than too hot any day.

Shortly after he settled into bed, the sound of a door opening told Shadow that Annie had decided to visit. Suddenly, he wasn't tired any more. Nighttime visits had become rare, but Shadow loved them all the same. When he rested his head on Annie's lap and listened to her bedtime stories, he didn't feel like he was in the shelter anymore. He felt like he was *home*.

Shadow stood and limped to the front of his kennel. He listened to Annie's familiar footsteps and her hushing of barking dogs until suddenly, she was there.

"Hi, buddy!" Annie whispered as she slipped into the kennel. "How are you?"

Shadow responded by licking the snow from Annie's gloves, which made her laugh.

"Come on, let's go sit down." Annie sat near the edge of Shadow's bed, leaning her back against the wall. Shadow plopped down next to her and rested his chin on her leg.

"I wanted to see you tonight." Annie suddenly sounded tired, although Shadow wasn't sure why. She had sounded that way a lot recently, her typical light and joy tempered by fatigue. It wasn't the kind of tired that could be fixed by sleeping, but a weariness that comes from having your hopes dashed to pieces too many times. Shadow understood that feeling, but it didn't make sense for Annie to be like that. He was old, but she was barely even out of her puppy years.

"Tomorrow, it's been a year since you first came here, buddy. For what it's worth, it's been the best year I've had working here. I've only been here for two, but you know.

"I always tell Cam and Ollie about you when I go home, just like I tell you about them. I wish you three could have been friends. I'm so sorry. I tried talking to my landlord again, but I knew she wouldn't allow it. And I called all around and asked everyone I know and it just…" she trailed off. Annie sounded ready to cry, but she managed to keep her voice level. "It just isn't fair."

After a long pause, Annie said, "Hey, listen Shadow. Tomorrow you're going to have to go see Anthony, okay? You remember Anthony, right?"

Shadow looked up and used a hind leg to scratch his neck. *Of course he knew Anthony. Had Annie forgotten that?* She seemed upset about something, but Shadow couldn't figure out what it was. Humans could be incredibly confusing at times. *What was the big deal about going to see Anthony?*

"You're going to have to be brave, okay buddy?"

Shadow rested his head on Annie's lap again and she put a hand on his neck, gently scratching his favorite spot. They waited in silence for a while, and Shadow was nearly asleep when Annie spoke again.

"The snow's really picking up out there. I guess we'll have to make sure you get to go play in it on your walk tomorrow, huh? I wish I loved the snow the way you do, buddy. It looks like fun. I wonder what you were like as a puppy when you saw your first snow. Do you remember

Penny, my dog I told you about? The one who thought she was a cat? She loved the snow almost as much as you. Her first snow was a big one, at least a foot deep. We let her outside to play in it, and it was almost like she was scared of it at first."

Annie laughed, and Shadow was glad that she seemed to have cheered up. *Did he make her as happy as she made him?* He certainly hoped so.

"I guess it *was* almost up to her neck. But she got used to it. We even had to carry her back inside at the end of the day, otherwise I don't think she ever would have come in. She bounded all over the yard, hopping as high as she could to get over the top of the snow. And every time she came up to a big drift, she'd attack it. Just take huge bites out of it until it was gone. And then she'd look at us, all proud of herself, like she'd saved us from some monster.

"I bet you did something cute during your first snow, too. Is that true, buddy?" Annie ruffled the fur on top of Shadow's head, but quickly smoothed it back out again.

It took several moments for Shadow to conjure up the memory, but he had no intention of ever forgetting his first snow. He had gone out into the yard and barked excitedly at every snowflake that passed his face. He'd also managed to trip over his own paws and fall face-first into the snow at one point. Brian only got him inside again with promises of food, which no smart puppy would ever turn down.

"Speaking of snow, did I tell you how I did in my race a few days ago? I don't usually run races, but my sister wanted to and we're only together a few days each year. For some reason, it's way easier to run when Ollie's pulling me down the sidewalk. Probably because he's doing most of the forward moving, and I'm just trying not to fall.

"Anyway, it was this 5k on Christmas morning. They called it the Christmas Classic. Creative, right? My goal was just to go the whole way without walking, but I actually ran pretty fast! I placed ninety-fifth, which doesn't sound that good except there were four hundred people in the race, so I beat a lot of them! Pretty good, right? They had breakfast burritos at the finish line, but none of them were vegan so we just went to the store and bought a whole pack of blueberry bagels, three for each of us…"

Shadow's eyelids grew heavy and he eventually fell asleep, though he was aware of Annie's voice in the background. He couldn't remember exactly what time she left, only that when she did, she gently transferred his head from her lap to the bed and gave his nose a kiss.

He didn't see her again until late the next morning, when she appeared outside of his kennel with a leash. Instantly awake, Shadow stood and shook himself before the word walk even left Annie's mouth. Very few things were more exciting than exploring fresh snow.

Shadow limped all throughout the walk, but stiff joints would *never* stop him from playing in the snow. Every time he spotted a deep drift, he pulled against his leash until Annie followed. Then he'd plow through the drift with his chest, only stopping when the snow became too packed to push or when a laughing Annie pulled him back to the path.

At a point that wasn't very far from the shelter— maybe a few hundred yards—Shadow decided it was time to stop, knowing he'd be too tired if he pushed any farther. Annie knelt and scratched Shadow's favorite spot, which felt absolutely delightful. He rolled onto his back and waited for Annie to scratch his belly, but instead she reached into her pocket and produced a roll. "Just for you, buddy!"

The roll was flaky and soft, squishing between Shadow's teeth like a much tastier version of his tennis ball. It was gone within seconds. When he finished, Annie stood.

"Ready to go back?" she asked.

Shadow answered by staring up at her with that open-mouthed smile, tongue flopping out of his mouth. Once they were inside again, Shadow waited patiently while Annie hung her coat and stomped off her boots. He shook the snow from his back, spraying a fine powder all over the floor. Little bits of snow stuck to Shadow's collar even after he shook himself a second time, but he decided not to worry about them.

Annie led him down the hall and into the adjacent hallway. When they walked right past the door that led to the kennels, Shadow gave Annie a questioning look. The layout of the building wasn't exactly straightforward, and he wondered if Annie had gotten lost. Humans did that sometimes, since they lacked any kind of decent sense of smell.

"It's time for you to go see Anthony now," Annie explained. She led Shadow around another corner, stopping in front of the doors to the vet's room. Shadow was surprised to see Kim waiting there with Anthony, but the sight of her excited him all the same. She stepped forward, resting a hand on top of Shadow's head.

"I just wanted to say goodbye, Shadow. I wish I could take you. I'm sure we all wish we could. It was wonderful to know you." She laughed. "I'm not going to forget that time you pulled me into a snowdrift, though! But really, you're such a good dog."

She told him goodbye a second time and then disappeared around a corner in the hallway. Shadow wasn't sure *where* Kim was going, but he hoped she'd have fun there, and was glad she came to say goodbye. It made him sad when people left without saying goodbye.

Annie knelt in front of Shadow again, and he licked the tip of her nose. She laughed. "You're so good, buddy. I'm going to miss you."

Shadow cocked his head, confused. *Why was everyone telling him goodbye? Where were they all going?*

Annie's hands found the sides of Shadow's neck. Sighing, she pressed her forehead against his, just like she had on that rainy day so long ago. Something about the way she smelled told Shadow she was upset, but he couldn't think of any reason why. By the time Annie pulled away again, tears had welled up in her eyes.

"I'm sorry—" a sniffle interrupted her, and the tears spilled over. "I told myself I wasn't going to cry. Guess that's not the only thing I was wrong about, huh? I'm so sorry.

"Listen buddy, I know I never got to take you home, but I want you to know you're a part of my family. You're one of my babies, just like Cam and Ollie."

Annie let out another shaky sigh and smoothed Shadow's fur down. "You be good, okay Shadow? You're a good boy. Don't ever forget it."

She nodded at Anthony, who gave her a wan smile and took the leash. As Shadow followed Anthony into the vet's room, he glanced back, suddenly worried he might never see Annie again. His friend stood alone in the hallway, arms crossed and eyes red. She met Shadow's gaze and waved, forcing a weak smile. Then the door swung shut, and Annie was gone.

Chapter 16

"Alright, Shadow," said Anthony in his slow, gentle voice.

He wrapped his strong arms beneath Shadow's body and hoisted him onto an exam table. At Anthony's request, Shadow settled into a lying position. The metal surface of the table was cool against his side, but nothing like the cool of fresh snow. The table was a sterile, unfeeling sort of cool, like floor of a kennel after cleaning.

The vet disappeared for a moment, but Shadow could hear him nearby, rummaging around in search of something. When he'd been younger, the thought of a vet searching for some tool out of sight would have been terrifying. He trusted them now though. *Be still, cooperate, and it'll be over soon.*

Anthony returned with a set of hair trimmers and gently took hold of Shadow's forelimb. "Alright Shadow, don't be scared. Just a little haircut."

Shadow had been to the groomer even more times than he'd been to the vet, so haircuts didn't scare him even a little bit. He waited patiently while Anthony trimmed a small patch of fur from a forelimb.

"Good boy." Anthony shut the trimmers off and gave Shadow's leg a light squeeze, just above the elbow. "There's a good vein," he said, and reached over to pat Shadow's side. "Good boy. Nice and calm. Good boy."

Annie's voice surprised them both. "Um…"

Shadow and Anthony both looked to the door to see Annie standing in front of it. She seemed a little embarrassed, but her face melted into tears again as she moved closer to the table.

"I'm sorry," she said to Anthony. "I thought I couldn't bear to watch, but—I have to be here for him.

"Sorry," she said again, wiping the tears away from her eyes. "I know we're supposed to handle it better than this and I need to get used to it but—"

"That's fine." Anthony put a reassuring hand on Annie's arm. "None of us ever get used to it. I'm sure Shadow would be happy to have you here with him."

Annie came around the table and cradled Shadow's head in her arms. Shadow *was* glad to have her there. He would always be glad to be with Annie, anywhere. He didn't live with her, but as far as he was concerned, Annie was his human. She had been for a long time. He wanted to tell her not to cry, and that everything was going to be okay. He wanted to sit up and lick the tears from her face, but just then, Anthony took hold of his arm again. It was time to be still. Anthony inserted a catheter, and the needle's bite hurt more than Shadow remembered. He was good though, and didn't budge.

Annie choked back a sob, and Shadow licked the tears from her face as soon as Anthony released his arm. He didn't understand why she was crying so much, but he *did* know exactly how to comfort her.

Annie laughed, like she always did when Shadow licked away her tears. One of her hands pushed him back down, but it was a gentle push. "Thanks buddy," she said. "You're so good. You have to stay down now though, okay?"

Shadow obeyed, and Annie resumed cradling his head in one arm. With her free hand, she smoothed out the fur on his neck with long, gentle strokes.

Anthony returned to the side of the table, holding a syringe. "You know he won't feel a thing," he said. He waited for Annie to nod, then said, "Alright Shadow. Nice and still. Good boy."

Something icy flowed through the catheter and into Shadow's vein, but he remained still, just like Anthony told him to.

Annie's face was close to his ear. "I'm right here, buddy." Her fingers worked at the buckle on his collar, and suddenly the collar fell away.

"I'm never going to forget about you," she said. "Don't forget about me when you're in heaven, okay?" And then the tears came again all at once, as if some dam in Annie's eyes had opened. Just as the tears flowed, cool fluid continued to flow into Shadow's veins. *That was alright*, he thought sleepily. *He didn't mind the cold.*

He wanted to lick Annie's tears away again, but his mind suddenly felt foggy, his thoughts slow. Annie's voice grew a little more distant. "Goodbye buddy. I love you."

Whatever fluid had been flowing through the catheter ceased to flow, and Anthony pulled the empty syringe away. Shadow's eyelids suddenly felt heavier than they ever had before, so he allowed them to shut.

Annie's crying became more distant. Her words grew muffled. Something about not being able to save him. Shadow tried to sit up and lick away her tears, but his head was just too heavy. His thoughts were sluggish, but he realized it was time to go to sleep. Sleep would be good. Slowly, he allowed the full weight of his head to rest on Annie's arm. *Annie. His best friend.* Her distant sobs grew heavier, but through the fog, Shadow managed to make sense of what she was saying: "I love you, buddy," repeated over and over. Shadow would have wagged his tail, if only it wasn't so hard to move. That was all he'd ever wanted. To be loved.

He stayed awake just long enough to hear Annie's last words, whispered in his ear.

"You're finally going home."

Millions of animals will be euthanized in shelters this year.

Some of them are waiting for new homes right now, just like Shadow. If you would have saved his life, please go save one of theirs.

Hey there! Thank you for reading *Shadow*. If you enjoyed this book, please consider posting a short review on Amazon and telling a friend. Sharing an author's work is the best compliment you can give, and your time is very much appreciated! You can also find me on Facebook for updates on future work: facebook.com/arisfortheanimals

Thanks!

Hey, it's me, Aris! I felt weird writing my own author bio in third person, so I decided not to do that. Besides, it feels a little impersonal.

Anyway, before I tell you a little about myself, I'd like to acknowledge a few important people who helped make this book happen. My partner, Erica, who offered me her constant love and support. Erica and my mother, Renee, who muddled through unpolished versions of this book to help me make it better. Love & Second Chances, for the important rescue work they do, and V-dog for their support. Kira, who never got the chance to grow old, but served as an inspiration for so many of Shadow's habits and behaviors. Kashi, my wonderful cover model. And God, to whom I prayed for help with my writing every step of the way.

I'm an activist and author living in Colorado. I love spending time with my friends of every species, and I'll never turn down a slice of vegan pizza. I'm on a mission to use books to make the world a better place for animals, and I'd love it if you'd join me! Please, if this book had an impact on you, take action. Adopt a senior dog or donate to rescue organizations. Challenge the idea that animals are disposable rather than thinking, feeling beings who deserve our loyalty and respect. And be sure to keep an eye out for future work from me. You can learn more on my website, arisaustin.wixsite.com/authorforanimals or on my Facebook page at facebook.com/arisfortheanimals.

See you around!

CPSIA information can be obtained
at www.ICGtesting.com
Printed in the USA
LVOW11s2314250417
532191LV00001B/142/P